W9-BXM-068

THE BOOK OF
TORMOD

A TEMPLAR'S GIFTS

KAT BLACK

SCHOLASTIC PRESS
NEW YORK

Book design by Christopher Stengel

Library of Congress Cataloging-in-Publication Data

Black, Kat.
   A Templar's gifts / Kat Black. — 1st ed.
     p. cm. — (The book of Tormod)
Summary: As the Chosen, Tormod knows he will have all the Gifts heaven and earth can bestow, but he still struggles to gain control of his visions and powers as men of the French King seek the relics he is bound to protect.
                    ISBN-13: 978-0-545-05675-5
1. Templars — History — Juvenile fiction. [1. Templars — Fiction.   2. Knights and knighthood — Fiction.   3. Middle Ages — Fiction.   4. Clairvoyance — Fiction.
5. Apprentices — Fiction.   6. Adventure and adventurers — Fiction.   7. Christian life — Fiction.]   I. Title.
   PZ7.B52896Tg 2011
   [Fic] — dc22
                                                                        2010016913

      10 9 8 7 6 5 4 3 2 1   11 12 13 14 15
                    Printed in the U.S.A.   23
                    First edition, April 2011

To all of my Guardian Angels

Sometimes I think of the words of a great man I knew, and believe that the future is changeable. Like a boulder dropped into a stream, diversion can disrupt the future that might be, for the one that is meant to be. Other times I think that I am nothing more than the weeds washed up on the shore by the great tides of Mother Earth. It matters not. I am a Templar's apprentice in deed, if not in word.

It was difficult to move back into the life of before. I tried to be as I was once, just the seventh son of a large family, but things had changed in me, and around me . . .

From the journal of Tormod MacLeod,
Scribed in the month of August 1307

PART ONE

AWAKENED

"Tormod?"

Rain beaded cold on my skin. Thunder rumbled through my chest. White-hot light blinded my eyes as a jagged rent tore the black of a velvet sky. The creeping shape of men flashed in the glare. Their dark intent shimmered in my mind.

"He's here. Quickly." The voice rasped. My heart beat furiously as I strained to see.

"Tormod!" My mam's voice was close, like the man from the vision, but I could spare her no attention. I was frightened to the core and growing more so as the moments passed. I could not break the hold.

Water crashed down over me, and the vision dropped away as if it had never been. In its place, confusion and fear remained. The room was dim and I shook with cold. A strange and awkward weight pinned my legs and panic unfurled within me. From all around the room, emotion lashed my unprotected mind.

Focus. I whispered the command silently to myself,

seeking the stillness within as I had been taught, but the feel of my sight was distant.

Ground. The lifeblood of the land trickled slowly beneath my feet. I reached for it, as I had so many times before. Yet only the barest tendril responded, slipping into my body to dull the crush of my family's fear and worry. Still, I was strengthened by it. Breath eased in my chest, and I was able to continue gathering the power that came sluggishly at my command.

Shield. With great effort, I forced the power I had called outward. It pressed against the inside of my skin, and a thin, soft barrier to the world beyond slid into place. The chaos dropped away.

The commands for shielding had worked, but these protections would not hold for long. I had to escape. Already the cry of my sister threatened my new control. Yet the sound brought with it memory, and for that I was grateful.

"I'm sorry, Caro," I whispered, kissing the top of her head and squeezing her slight frame as she shivered. I'd been telling a story about the lands I had seen on my journey. Caro was six and could never get enough of the tales.

I had been talking about the sky and the way the top of the mountain had stretched clear through the clouds, but, in the midst of my description, a vision had descended and I dropped hard into the middle of a thunderstorm. I had no idea how long I sat frozen, nor what had happened while my family looked on.

It wasn't the first time I had lost myself in the visions. There had been several incidents since my return, but this was different. This was worse. Usually the presence of the bairns kept me grounded, but even their innocence and purity, which I usually found balming, were of no help. I glanced over to Torquil and caught the awkwardness of his stare. I turned quickly away, but his animosity seemed to follow.

"Hush ye now," said my mam, lifting the bairn. "Everything's fine."

Caro's eyes were lost and frightened and I felt a beast. Without thought, I reached for the power of the land to soothe her fear, but it leapt at my call, far more strongly than I expected. I shoved it back down into the earth, alarmed. I could not afford to work with it when I had so little control.

"Let's get ye dried. 'Tis just a puddle. Ye'll be set aright in no time." She turned to fetch new clothes for Caro and over her shoulder spoke to me. "There's a sark on the wash line, Tormod. Be sure to hang that one in its place. James, put down some rushes and soak up the water. Torquil, build up the fire."

I pulled the sopping material over my shoulders and hurried out the door. Lord, how would I explain this one? I could scarcely credit what had happened myself.

I'd been deep in a vision and my mam had upended a bucket of water on me. Things had gone from bad to worse in the short time I'd been home.

Home. Why had I longed so badly to be here? During the endless trek from the caves, over the sea in the merchant ship, it was all I could think of. And yet, now that I was here, the need to leave again struck me stronger than ever before. I no more fit in now than when I'd left.

The sark made a slapping sound as I slung it over the line. It reminded me of the crack of thunder and the men in the vision. Who were they and why was I seeing them?

The sun was weak, its rays barely warming the dew on the last of the season's grass. August was near at end, and the days had been unseasonably cold and damp. The cloth of my spare sark was stiff beneath my fingers — there had been no summer breeze to dry it soft. I gave it a good shake to knock away anything sleeping within and shrugged into it as bile washed at the back of my throat, and I felt a shakiness in my legs that had not been there before. The visions always weakened me. I sat on a stump of rotted oak, letting the images roll over in my memory. Who were they and what were they seeking? I prayed that it was not the Holy Vessel.

The ancient carving and beautiful bowl were no longer my responsibility, and yet I worried still. I'd done what the Templar Alexander had charged and delivered both pieces to the Abbot at Balantrodoch.

The memory of that morning still had the power to warm me, even on so cold a day as this. When I drew the carving from my sack and placed the sacred bowl into the Lady's upturned hands, I had the feeling that I had become a part of something special, sacred, and holy. In the dim light of the study, with the heat and strength of the carving's light pulsing in my hands, I told the Abbot all that had befallen the Templar and me.

To say that he had been stunned would be putting it mildly. That we would be drawn halfway around the world following visions set forth by an ancient carving; that the King of France would set a legion of soldiers and mercenaries on our trail; and that I alone would escape the ambush that had taken the life of the Templar Alexander to return to the Abbot with an artifact of so great a power that it must be kept secret from the whole of humanity was astounding even to me.

I squirmed in my seat, thinking on the Abbot's response. The elder Templar leader had dropped to his knees and reverently whispered that I was the Protector, the Chosen of the Lord. He had actually crossed himself, taken my hand, and sworn fealty to me. "From this day ever onward I swear allegiance to ye, Tormod MacLeod. The light has chosen ye for its own. Be ever vigilant o' those who would subvert it for darkness."

"Tormod! Stop yer gawpin'. I'll no' be doin' yer chores while ye sit about." I glared at Torquil.

Protector. Chosen. I scoffed at the idea. Not chosen at home, unless it was to protect sheep and bairns. No. Here I was just Tormod, the odd one, the lad no one could truly reconcile.

I stood and turned back toward the hut as the wind whipped up over the hillside. A shiver slid through me, and I quickly cast about for the source of my sudden apprehension.

"Tormod! Da could be here any time," he warned.

"Aye. I'm coming." *Da*, I thought, sighing. I would need an explanation of what had gone on before he arrived. All of this proved once again that the only place that I should be was with the Order. Da, though, had other ideas. Things between us, since my return, had not been the way they once were.

DREAMS AND VISIONS

The battle raged around me and I was covered in blood. Soldiers were advancing. I tried to stand, to run. Off in the distance, there came a flash of white. I turned, stunned. Riding toward me was the Templar Alexander, his mighty sword cleaving a path to my side.

I woke suddenly, thrust from the dream into the black of the hut, yet his image remained strong in my mind. I held it close, the joy of seeing him warring with the sadness of losing him. *A dream,* I told myself. Dreams did not come true. Visions did, at least in their fashion. The worst of these had come to me in the very beginning. I had seen blood, the blood of the Templar Alexander Sinclair, seep from a cross of red. My heart wrenched at the memory.

This vision had come true, though I had tried with all my might to avert it. My friend and teacher was dead. There would be no reunion, no one to save me. I was alone. A sob escaped without my willing it.

"Tormod?" My mam's voice slid softly across the darkened space. I felt her concern as if it was my own. Its strength was stifling, swelling the very air around me.

"Ye're home an' safe, Tormod," she whispered. "It's over, lad."

I reached quickly for my plaid and boots. She didn't understand. It was not over. It would never be over. Carrying my things and working hard not to step on the sleeping bodies of my family, I made for the door.

"Tormod?"

Her fear surged through me and I stumbled. "I just

need air," I gasped, willing my voice to sound calm and my movements to appear smooth. The hard cut of her feelings was too much to bear.

It had been this way from the moment I'd returned. Being near people was impossible. The power of the Holy Vessel had opened my mind to the edges of their thoughts and feelings. Their sadness, worry, anger, and fear became my own.

This by itself would have been bad enough, but I found out quickly that when my own emotions mixed with theirs, both multiplied in me. It felt like a dagger being shoved deep into my mind and heart, and each feeling added was a turn of the blade.

My ragged breath hung on the air as I made my way over the rocky land. The damp clung to my skin. I hurried to don my plaid and step into my boots. It was odd that even after all this time, the feel of my left boot, looser than the right, surprised me.

It was the first of the many things that had changed when I left home. I'd lost two toes to the freezing sickness. At the time I thought it the most devastating thing I might ever endure. I was my da's runner. I delivered messages from one end of the village to the other and I feared I'd no longer be able to. It was a terrible thing, but I had seen true suffering, lost so much in the way of friends, that now it seemed as nothing in comparison.

My mam's worry reached out to me through the heavy stone walls of the hut and down the slope to where I sat near the road. After a moment it came on stronger, and I knew she stood at the window with the flap of the shutter pulled back.

There was nothing I wanted more than to walk away from the hut and her eyes, down to the beach and off. Distance alone would break the hold that kept me shivering, but I would not do that to her. Mam had enough to worry over without my adding to it. I had caused her enough heartbreak for a lifetime.

Autumn would soon set in, and the winter freeze would follow fast. There would be fewer trips to fish. Food had been set aside for the change in season, but it was less than usual. Fishing had not been plentiful this summer.

My insides churned with the memory of a conversation I had with the Templar so long ago. I'd asked if the village would be punished because I had not provided the flint and tinderbox to start the Beltane fire on time. I had chosen instead to deliver the message that began this strange path, my fate.

The Templar told me he thought God was not a vengeful being and that if the crops did not grow or the fish were few, it was because the growing and feeding cycles had somehow changed.

I wanted to believe him then. I wanted it to be true now, but more than ever I worried. I felt the stares and blame whenever the topic of a lean winter arose. The whisper of accusation shouted at the edge of their thoughts. It made me want to lash out, to scream that they could not understand what it was like. But I could tell them nothing. How could I openly admit that I could read their minds?

Stray bits of leaves and dirt swirled past me toward the beach. I focused on the pattern of power, saw the pulse of the air that lifted them and used my gift to shift their course. The wind turned, whipping with much more force than I had intended, and a small stripling uprooted under the onslaught. It lay on the ground, fragile and broken.

I dropped the whisper with a strangled cry and hurried to the plant. *Lord, I apologize. I am no' worthy o' yer gifts.* Shame scalded me. The Templar had taught me to do many things with the power, and I had excelled in the lessons. Yet now, even the simplest reach went horribly wrong. I knelt and dug my hands into the soil, saying the prayer to Our Lady that the stripling might once again take root in the soil.

Behind me, Mam's worry grew, and our feelings combined, spiraling into a frenzy. I called upon the shielding commands, but instead of relief, the horizon suddenly tilted. Before my eyes, the village square, the kirk, and the scattering of huts grew hazy. Blinking, I tried to push the strangeness away, but no amount of effort changed what I saw. The familiar landscape had vanished. Trees and forest crowded the space, their tangle of rotted gray limbs askew and covered by a sickly green moss.

The healer in me felt the wrongness of the scene. The pulse of the land's power was in a tangle. The lifeblood of the trees, the sap, was thick and congealed. I saw pools of stagnant muck leaching from the roots.

Horrified, I reached with my mind to heal the damage and suddenly it all dropped away. Quickly I laid my hand on the ground, puzzled when the pure and perfect thrum of the land rose to my touch. I sifted a handful of dirt through my fingers, dispersing the power and murmuring a silent prayer of thanks, wondering what the oddity meant.

I felt the weight of Mam's gaze, though she stood in the dark of the hut. Her mind had settled. The raw fear she had been sending my way was now curiosity.

It was an emotion, at the moment, I didn't mind sharing. What was I to think of *this* vision? I wished, not for the first time, that the Templar were here with me. I knew that although he might not have the answer, I would be the better for talking it out with him.

With a sigh I trudged up the slope. Mam had returned to her pallet.

A RECKONING

Days passed with little or no trouble from my lapse into the vision state, but my da had been out with his crew then. He and my brothers had arrived this morning and I had managed to avoid him up until now — no easy task.

I felt his approach as I cleaned the muck in the animal byre and bolted out back and up the slopes as fast as my legs would carry me. I was safe from confrontation, but I'd only made it as far as the first of our sheep grazing in the rough, when a strong stir of emotion hit me hard. *Think o' nothing*, I chanted to myself. *Hear only yer own thoughts.*

A ewe wandered close and I latched on to her soft nape, trying to block out all but the simple essence of the animal. Mam's and Da's words and feelings came to me nevertheless.

"I don't know what happened. One moment he was tellin' the bairn a story, an' the next he was sittin' an' starin', stuck with a terrified expression on his face." I heard Mam all too clearly. It made me ill to listen to them this way. I used to do it for fun, to get information I would not otherwise be privy to. But now, as it was not something I could control, I hated it.

14

"I'm worried for the lad. I've heard tales o' this." Da's words were as clear as if he stood beside me. "The death o' his friend has unhinged him."

My throat tightened at the thought, wondering if he was right.

"Mayhap, then, he should be with the Templars. Their healers can help," said my mam quietly.

I was shocked. Mam was championing my going to the Order.

"I've told ye I will no' speak o' this again. He is where he belongs, here at home with his family," said Da firmly. A swirl of anger rolled off of him. Mam's frustration was rising. Their emotions were within me, growing. My head ached. My guts heaved. I huddled against the ewe but could find no relief.

Lord, please, take this gift from me. I don't want it. My prayer was answered with a shift in the land's current. It swirled, buffeting me with comfort, stripping their conversation from my mind and reach.

Though the gray light of day slipped to a charcoal night, I remained on the slopes until it grew too cold to bear any longer, thinking about how best to deal with Da. I didn't want to answer questions about what had happened. It was not as if I could give him the answers he sought. He'd think me mad.

With a sinking heart, I realized he probably already did. It was something I wondered about myself. What was happening to me? I needed the Order, but the Templars had never called for me. I'd done my part by finding the Holy Vessel, whisking it out of the country beneath the very nose of those who sought it, and delivering it home to Scotia. Their part was to take me in and train me as a Templar. The Abbot had promised.

But for the whole of a moon's turn I had wandered these hills, tending sheep and watching the days seep one into the next, waiting for the summons. Every morning I prayed for some understanding about why they had not come for me. Never an answer came.

"Well, I'll no' be waiting forever," I said aloud to the sheep. "If they won't call for me, I will go to them and demand that they take me in." Once uttered, I knew the rightness of it. Staring off over the slopes, I felt small and very much alone. Leaving was my only hope.

CONFRONTED

The smell of the tallow was strong and I watched the thick, oily smoke inch its way toward the roof beams.

The flame's small flicker did little to light the dimness of the hut. I sat on my pallet, pleating the worn edge of a blanket with my fingers, wishing to be anywhere else.

"Has this happened before?" Da asked. He was hunkered down before me, not restlessly pacing as was his wont a moment ago. I preferred the former to this unswerving attention.

I kept my eyes averted, staring up into the corner so as not to make contact, fighting the feelings he projected. It was as if a weight pressed hard on my heart. "No, Da. I didn't hear Mam calling me. I was thinking o' something else."

"What the devil could ye be thinking?" he demanded. His voice was like the crack of a whip and I flinched. "Ye were in the midst o' a story."

"I don't know. Just what I was going to say next," I stammered, lying. It was another reason I would not look at him. I hated lying. It was not right and I was no good at it.

The questioning had been going on for an age. I wracked my mind for something I could tell him. "My mind drifted an' the next thing I knew Mam had doused me." That was the truth and I met his eyes squarely as I said it.

It didn't work. Da was not to be put off and adamant to get to the bottom of the trouble. "Tormod, I know that ye miss yer friend, an' what ye've been through would hurt even a full-grown man, but it would help if ye talked about it."

That was the last thing I could take. "There's nothing to talk about!" I shouted, reeling under the press of his emotion as well as my own. "Leave off, man! I'm no' a bairn."

Da's fist bunched and his stare was a hard, stone-cold thing. I'd crossed a line I should not have. "Watch yerself, lad." His voice was dead-calm quiet. "I've allowed as much leave as ye best be taking, or ye'll find yerself bent over the fence post facing my strap like a bairn."

I leapt up and pushed past him, fleeing the hut as if all the demons of the underworld panted at my heels. He did not follow, but his anger and hurt did.

The very next day I began stowing things in a nook beneath a jut of rock, high on the hillside. I knew what a trek across the land entailed, and though I only intended to go as far as the preceptory, I had long ago determined never again to be caught without the supplies I needed to travel.

One by one, I smuggled blankets out under my plaid. Old, worn, and stained from the bairns, I knew they would not be missed. An old flint accompanied bits of dried fish from the root cellar, and a small supply of carrots and potatoes followed. I took an old skin as well and filled it with water from the stream. I had my dagger, two extra pair of breeks, and a sark, just in case I had need of them.

In all, it took near on a week for me to gather everything I wanted. Once I'd made up my mind to go, I found I could barely wait.

That night, only the small glow of the cook fire broke the black of the hut's interior. The soft sigh of my sleeping family shushed like the sway of the birch outside. Da was the last to retire. We'd been treading lightly around each other since the argument. I'd not apologized, nor had he.

I sat up slowly, craning to see through the gloom. Lumps and piles of sleeping bodies were all about, on pallet and floor. Pushing aside my blanket, I felt for my supplies. Boots and plaid, both readily at hand. I'd already wriggled into my clothes beneath the covers. It had taken forever and my heart had nearly burst from my chest with worry that someone might hear and take note.

Now, silently, I crept from my place, whispering the barest push of exhaustion to those sleeping around me. Though I had no business using the power, I could not afford to take chances. A wave of dizziness washed over me and I held my breath, waiting for it to pass. No one stirred. I reached for the door and looked back only once. "Farewell," I whispered. "I love ye."

Tears blurred my sight as I stepped out into the night. The wind cut hard into the chinks and corners unprotected by my plaid, and the slope was sharp beneath my legs. *I can do this,* I told myself. *I've done it before.*

As I climbed, night sat heavy on my shoulders. I was much better without light now than I once had been. During my last trek, the merest grouping of shadows had frightened me. Tonight I moved with purpose, behind the hut and up over the rocky landscape. It took only moments to locate the gap in the rocks. My old linen sack sat beneath the overhang just where I'd placed it. With the determination to be gone, I purposefully reached down into the blackened space.

"What d'ye think ye're doin'?" A heavy hand clamped down on my shoulder and my heart nearly leapt from my chest. Then all at once the night faded to a deep dark black. I was no longer there. Hard stone pressed against my cheek and pain seared my skin. The crack of a whip and the harsh wheeze of my breath sounded in my ears, and in my mind there was a horrible keening, echoing in the darkness and tearing at my heart.

"Why are ye skulking about in the dead o' night?" Torquil's voice cut away the vision but not the horror. I gasped, breathing heavily, confused and frightened.

"Torquil?" I shuddered, desperate to press the memory away, to get out of here as fast as possible. "Go away! Leave me be."

"What are ye doin', Tormod? I'll no' ask ye again." His voice was loud. My ears hurt. The sack in my hands was heavier than before, and I slung it wearily over my shoulder.

"Please. I don't have the strength for this. I've got to go," I protested. "I dare no' stay a moment longer," I said quietly. "It's dangerous to the family, an' to me as well." It was more than I wanted to say. They were coming for me.

Torquil did not shift a muscle, just stared as if he would never move. I made to go around him and he stepped into my path. I shoved him with all of the built-up frustration and fear I'd been holding. He stumbled back a step.

"There are things that ye don't know, things I can never tell anyone, that happened while I was away," I snapped. "Don't ye see, I'm no' the same inside. Ye know what I was when I left."

This reached him. His eyes dropped. He knew well what I meant and it bothered him still. The rift between us grew deeper and wider.

I'd seen the death of the da of one of his friends, and Torquil let it be known. It had not gone well for me after that.

"It's worse now, Torquil. I have to go, before something happens." I'd no sooner spoken when . . .

Dust rose in a cloud. Thundering hooves. The great wooden gate. The Abbot's study.

"Who was the boy traveling with Alexander Sinclair?"

"I know no such boy."

My knees nearly buckled as the vision slid away. It was too much. My heart pounded, and I felt like I was going to vomit. "They hunt me. I can't go to the preceptory," I mumbled.

My panic reached Torquil. "Who, Tormod? Who?" His fingers dug into my shoulders and I gave up any effort to conceal the vision.

"Men o' the French King." The words tore from me. "They're coming!" My frightened gaze begged him to understand. "Torquil, don't try to stop me. They're killers an' they're looking for me. Go away. Go home." His stare was hard. He fought some internal war I did not have time for. I made to leave.

"We'll take the boat," he said, his words shocking me to the core.

"What? No," I protested. "I'll go alone. Da will kill ye if ye take the boat without permission." I started quickly down the slope but Torquil remained fast on my heels.

"If I don't do it, I could no' live with myself," he said almost so quietly I did not hear. The sound of our rushed steps echoed loud in the night. Tremors rippled along my spine as we bolted through the village, down to the water's edge. They could be here at any time. I could never tell with the visions.

OFF AGAIN

We were on my da's fishing boat and out into the harbor in barely a quarter the time that was usual. I stood at the bow, willing the boat to move faster, watching the edge of my world disappear yet again. The water was dark and choppy, and we dipped jerkily in the waves. I was frozen and my insides rocked with the ocean's movement. We were traveling as quickly as the wind might take us, but what if it was not enough?

Torquil manned the wheel while I watched, sick with fright as the shoreline disappeared in the darkness. Whether it was truly my own fear or the reflection of Torquil's, I didn't know.

"Where can ye hide?" he asked. Torquil's face was in shadow, but I knew it was taut with worry. His emotions were battering my own, making it difficult to think. It was all so confusing.

"I have a friend in Arbroath. If I can get there, he will take me in," I said grudgingly. I'd often thought of Bertrand, the Knight Templar with the gift of healing. He had cared for me when I lost my toes and promised to help if ever the need arose.

The wind tossed the ocean into a churning white froth. I felt the raw and ancient power of its depths, but took no pleasure in it. My thoughts were filled with the terror of the soldiers hunting me. The "need" had surely arisen.

"I know the place," said Torquil. He had made many trips along the coast over the years. As a senior fisher-man on my da's boats, he often plotted and sailed.

It was a long while until dawn. Only the steady mur-mur of the waves parting around the hull disturbed the peace of the night. I should have been asleep on my feet, but my body was strung tight. Hunched against the chill within and without, I stared up into the black and end-less sky, dotted by the pinpricks of light that spilled through from the heavens.

I drifted toward the mast and sat, watching the subtle movements of Torquil's hands and eyes. "I thank ye for helping me." It was nearly painful to say the words. We had been at odds for so long and our animos-ity toward each other was still fresh in my memory.

"Ye'll be facing a goodly portion o' chaff when ye return."

He ignored my words and fished a pouch from his sporran. "I saved my share of the haul this summer." His voice was low, but even soft conversation seemed loud on the water. "I thought to hold on to it in case I was able to get to market to buy Bridie a ring." My jaw dropped in shock. That he would give me money was nearly as surprising as the thought of him marrying. I looked for the lie. His eyes were far away. I could read nothing in their depths.

"I want ye to have it, Tormod," he said. "I don't like the idea of ye off with naught but the clothes on yer back an' that wee pack."

Another shock. "Ye've got plans for that coin," I gasped. "I canno' take it." I felt like it was a trap. "Ye've worked an' saved. Marriage?" I mumbled. "I can't even fathom it."

He smiled in his *I'm older and know something you don't* way. As usual it got under my skin, but I said nothing. "Go on an' take it." He tossed the pouch to the deck near my leg. "I've gotten on without a ring until now. I'll raise it again. Bridie'd no' care. She worried for ye long, ere ye went away."

Revelation on revelation. Bridie worried over my disappearance? The last I'd seen of her, she was mocking my hair and freckles. It was so small a thing now, I

25

wondered why it bothered me to begin with. "Why are ye helping me?" I said at last, nearly afraid to have mentioned it. In a small voice I said, "Ye hate me."

"Hate ye! Lord, whatever would give ye that ridiculous notion?" He seemed truly offended. I didn't know what to think.

"Come on, man," I exclaimed. "Ye've had no use for me for long an' away. Ye've been torturous since that day on the beach. I didn't plan on having that vision, nor did I expect you to tell Cormack I saw his da dead, Torquil. I was as shocked as ye were." I turned my eyes from his, still hurt by the memory.

The reference to it made him uncomfortable. "I just don't understand ye, Tormod. Why d'ye make trouble for yerself? Why can ye no' just do like the rest o' us? Be like the rest o' us?"

I let my head fall back against the wooden pole, looking to the heavens for guidance. "Don't ye think I wish that, Torquil? To be different than I am? Ye don't know what it's like to see things no one else does — to know things before they happen an' have no way to prevent them. This is no' something I chose or can control. The visions come to me. I don't court them. I don't even like them. But they are a part o' me, as much as the color of my eyes or hair."

He was quiet, brooding no doubt about my not falling in with his idea of what I should be or do. "What happened that day, Tormod? Where did ye go, an' why did ye wait so long to come back?"

My stomach heaved. I had not spoken to him directly about any of the things that had befallen me and I wasn't sure I wanted to. Fear and distaste were rolling off of him. "It's a long story," I said, sighing.

"Aye. Well, we seem to have a bit o' time. I've no' offered it much, but I've an ear to listen, if ye're of a mind to tell." His gaze was on me and I was torn. Torquil stood tall and strong at the wheel, and I missed the way it used to be between us. I told myself over and over again on the long journey home that I would someday win my brother back to my side. It hadn't happened yet. If I didn't take the chance now, might I lose it forever?

With a deep breath, I started the tale as it had been told to me by the Templar. "In the beginning there was one knight . . ."

The story crept out of me slowly, unfolding into the wee hours. The telling brought me back to places and faces I'd put aside. Being home had dulled the experiences into things less and less real as the days had gone by, but now they were back and the wonder of what I had seen and done was fresh and shocking, even to me.

Torquil listened with rapt attention, breaking in with questions from time to time. There were moments when he appeared doubtful, and others when he was truly astounded. And when I neared the end of my tale, I saw something in his eyes I had never expected to find. Dare I hope . . . respect?

"Ye escaped with an artifact o' great power and the soldiers of the King hunt ye," he said faintly. He shook his head as if to dispel the notion. "It's like a legend of old, Tormod. Are ye havin' me on?" He looked at me suspiciously.

"Truly," I insisted, "but my worries don't end there." Restless, I leapt up and started to pace, feeling the edginess within me churn. "There's an oddness that's come about, one that I canno' control. I've changed." I rubbed my eyes, feeling the throb of an aching head approach. My feelings were keyed to Torquil's and he was worried.

"Changed in what way?" he asked.

I was afraid to speak of my gifts. I'd long hidden them, especially at home. "Ye know I sometimes see things that have no' as yet happened?" I said. He nodded. I drifted to the rail, gripping it tightly, feeling Torquil's unease grow. "I have abilities now that I've never had before. I've been having visions about things happening beyond our croft and land, things that I think I should be making sense o', but I canno'."

He shifted, clearly uncomfortable. "I feel what others are feeling. Their emotions make me ill. Sometimes . . ." I hesitated. "I hear their thoughts in my head. I canno' shut them off or push them away. It's as if my mind is full to bursting an' I'm about to go mad."

He gaped. "That's what happened the other day, isn't it?" he asked. "Ye had another vision." His wariness of me peaked.

"Aye. It comes on suddenly an' I have no way to stop it. I've always believed that the visions come for a reason, to warn me that something is about to happen or to give me clues as to what I'm meant to do, but now I have all these other things going on and I don't think it's supposed to be that way."

"What ye said just now, about the visions telling ye something ye're meant to do. What did ye mean?" His eyes were fast on the horizon and yet I felt his attention, sharp and keen as he waited for an answer.

"Sometimes I try my best to change what I see. He told me I could," I said, remembering the many conversations we'd had about that very thing.

"Who, Tor?" he asked. Torquil hadn't called me that in a long while. It gave me a good feeling of home and the way it used to be.

"The Templar Alexander. He had the vision of what was, what would be, an' what could be. He said what I saw in the visions could be changed, because the future is no' yet determined." I sighed. "But I've no' seen any evidence o' this. I've tried, Torquil, so hard to change what I see, but near as I can tell I have no effect on the future whatsoever. Truly, sometimes I think I often *cause* what I see to happen."

My heart was near breaking at that thought voiced aloud. Had I caused the death of the Templar in trying to keep him from being killed?

A spike of strong emotion I could not name leapt from Torquil, cutting through my unhappiness. "I'm sorry I sent ye back for the tinderbox, Tor. If I hadn't, ye never would have gotten mixed up in all this trouble."

I was surprised by the vehemence in his voice. "Ye needn't worry over that, Torquil. I'd do it all again with no regrets if I had the chance."

He cradled the wheel. I could almost see the thoughts whirring in his mind, but only his feelings came across to me. He was anxious. "Is it safe?" he asked.

"Is what safe?"

"The artifact, the Holy Vessel ye found," he replied.

"Och, aye. The Order has it hidden away," I said, thinking of the Abbot and his assurances when I'd delivered it to him.

"But if your vision showed soldiers at the preceptory . . ." he said. I didn't remember saying that precisely.

" 'Tis safe," I said with conviction. "It has to be. My duty was to get it there. It's their responsibility now to keep it. They have a whole army to do it."

30

"Ye would know that more than any other," he said. I felt his confidence. It was a good and unexpected thing to have encountered in my brother after all I'd been through.

A soft wind swept the bow. The shush of the water, ever moving, drew me. Without reaching, the pure, clean life of the ocean came to me. Like the mist that coated my skin, it was fresh, cold, and invigorating.

The depths of the ocean called. And my mind was suddenly somewhere else.

"Come forward." The voice was melodic, and yet commanding. *"Tell me what you saw."*

"A light as like nothing I have ever encountered. The boy held it aloft and the hand of death struck any who advanced." The man's terror curled my guts.

"What was beyond the light? Surely you must be able to tell me something." His tone was scathing and the man flinched.

"I believe it was a vessel, my Liege. A base and a bowl of some sort. But the light was too bright to behold. I can tell you nothing more."

I snapped to as Torquil adjusted the sail. "Ye were drifting," he said apologetically. "I didn't mean to wake ye."

It only took a moment for my thoughts to readjust. The queasiness that always appeared in the wake of a vision roiled within me. They knew of the carving and bowl and I was their only link.

"Rest ye now, while ye can, Tormod. Ye will need yer strength when ye leave me. I'm here an' will take care of ye. Sleep."

I was bone weary. Even with the vision fresh and the fear of what was to come, I could barely keep my eyes open. And so when sleep stole over me, I gave myself up to the protection of my brother.

BOARDED

"Tormod!" Torquil's panic assaulted me before the words passed his lips. I woke quickly and struggled to rise, fighting his terror as well as my own.

"Prepare to be boarded." A strong voice cut across the bow.

"Your name is Dougal, an' mine is Ian," Torquil whispered anxiously. "We are MacDonalds from Inverness, returning from a sennight o' fishing." I nodded, barely able to think through the fear.

An enormous ship approached our vessel, its weight causing our deck to tilt precariously. A flood of emotion battered me — theirs, mine, Torquil's. Afraid of my lack of control, I quickly turned toward the water, reaching for its life and peace.

Across a gap in their rail, two large planks angled down to our deck from the other. The ocean was fading before my eyes and I fought the darkness creeping up on me.

"Your names." A burly soldier of mid-years boarded before the rest. His hair was dark and his scowl was frightening.

"Dougal and Ian MacDonald," Torquil answered. I heard the tremor in his voice and my eyes darted to the soldier. The man's narrow and suspicious gaze caught my own, and my backbone quivered. His look shifted then to Torquil, whose countenance gave nothing away.

"We were told this boat belongs to the MacLeod family. Do you deny this?" he demanded.

And the heat began to rise. I felt sweat gathering on my brow and running down the small of my back. The air wavered and I began to panic. *No. Not now*, I silently begged.

Soldiers riding hard along the road. A body, bundled in linen, draped over the back of one of the horses. The wind whipping. The covering torn back. The white, slack face of the Abbot bouncing with the jarring stride.

I came back to the sound of Torquil protesting the soldier now boarding our boat. My legs were weak and my body trembling. *Lord, please* . . . I begged, with my heart lodged somewhere behind my teeth as I reached for the strength of the sea. *These lads are no' the ones ye seek. Another boat on the horizon comes. Hurry.*

The whisper was difficult. The power was strong, and my efforts to hold it in check barely up to the task. Still, I focused the way the Templar had taught me.

"No. This boat belongs to my brother-in-law. We hail from Inverness," said Torquil. I could feel the fear making his heart pound and his hand tighten on the wheel.

The soldier's confusion wafted over me and I took hope from it. His eyes were slightly glazed, I noticed, and the tense alertness he had come aboard with had ebbed. I pushed again slightly, so that the wash of my suggestion would encompass the men behind him. *Another boat on the horizon.*

The man before me cocked his head, as if listening to something no one else heard. I forced the push a little harder, directly into his mind. A film of sweat broke out on his brow. I watched as he swayed then rushed to the rail.

Stock-still and terrified, I shifted my eyes to meet Torquil's. The man's retching was loud and worrisome. Moments stretched as my mind flit with panic. Our chances would be better if I continued the push, but with my power as unpredictable as it was, this man might die.

We had to get away. The longer he remained aboard, the less I would be able to do with the power. Already my body shook with fatigue. I softened the push and continued the whisper.

The soldier slowly straightened. His face was white and his clothing disheveled. Though I stared, he did not meet my eyes.

"Lieutenant! Come! There is another boat. These are not the ones we seek." The call from the ship was insistent. The man who had been vomiting turned away and, without a backward glance, hurried aboard his ship. The planks were quickly withdrawn and in moments they were cutting across the water.

I continued the faint whisper until they were a speck on the horizon, until the throbbing pressure of the power felt as if it would crush my head. Then, without warning, my knees buckled and the world began to tilt.

"Whoa! Hey!" Torquil scrambled to my side and helped me down to the deck. I was breathing shallowly and bright spots floated before my eyes. The wind blew cold, rippling across my face. The waves lifted the boat in a rolling gait that brought bile rushing to my throat. The Abbot had been taken. They knew of the Holy Vessel.

"How long to Arbroath?" I asked, gulping air, hoping to settle my stomach.

"Tomorrow afternoon at the earliest. Are ye all right?" he asked. I nodded and regretted the movement.

"How did ye turn them away?" he asked, adjusting the sail and moving back to the wheel. There was uneasiness in him and I knew it was his acknowledgment of the power use.

A heavy cloud moved directly above, making the sky just that much darker. I stared up at it, wondering how to answer. "Misdirection is the only way I can describe it. I suggested the possibility that a ship approached, that we were not their quarry. I only hope I didn't cause harm," I said. "I made him ill. My control is no' what ye'd call reliable."

"D'ye think they will come back?" Torquil asked.

"I don't know." My thoughts returned to the visions and the men who were hunting me. How had they tracked me so quickly? Would Arbroath be far enough away to hide?

"Get some more rest," he said. "Our course is straight. I can sail much of the day." Torquil was being uncharacteristically good to me, but I didn't have the strength to question it.

"Wake me if ye need anything," I said, lying down on a pile of crates that were stacked out of the wind. He nodded, and I closed my eyes and began to pray.

CLOSING THE DIVIDE

I slept for a long stretch, knowing that it was morning when the sun, weak as it was, lit the back of my eyes. The ocean was calm, and though the water's power should have soothed my ragged nerves, I was still jangling inside. Torquil yawned loudly and I pushed my way to wakefulness.

"Next time ye think to run away, mayhap ye might give me a bit o' warning. I could use my plaid." Torquil was tired and on the edge of snappish. I knew it to be from worry so I relieved him as quickly as I could.

"I'm sorry. Ye should have awakened me."

He grunted. "Ye needed the rest."

"Take a break," I said, handing him the sack of food and supplies and relieving him at the wheel. He took out a couple of bannocks and the water and made his way to the rail. Dark skies threatened off on the horizon. We were heading into a squall. The air was cold, and the wind would not be long away. The waves lengthened and deepened, lifting the boat and setting my insides churning. Restlessly I moved from one foot to the other and back again, wishing that it would even out.

"Do the visions always come true?" he asked. I was surprised that he would bring up the power.

"What I see comes to pass, but it's not always the way I think it will happen." I sighed, remembering. "I had a vision that the knight I traveled with would be killed." I took a deep breath, not wanting but needing to continue. "He was."

Torquil gasped.

I forced myself to go on. "But the circumstances that surrounded that vision were not what I had imagined them to be. I thought that one of the men who traveled with us would be the killer, but in the end it was he who interceded, an' tried his hardest to keep it from happening." My voice was leaden. "So. It's no' always the truth of the future that is seen. He was stabbed. He died. I saw his blood on the face of another, but if the vision had been wider I would have known that our friend was no murderer."

It was a thought that had grieved me for a long while. I hadn't trusted Ahram for any other reason than the flash of a vision and the idea that he was different from me. I felt ashamed.

"Still, it did come true. . . ." Torquil said. "Did ye warn him?" he asked a moment later.

"The Templar? I tried, but he would not hear a word o' it," I said. "He was adamant."

"If it were ye, would ye want to know?"

Torquil was acting strangely, and I found it hard to keep up. I thought about his question as I had done many times since I'd lost the Templar. I had once thought him daft for not wanting to know his fate, but now perhaps I understood better. "Seems no bargain," I said. "If ye can't change the outcome, what good is it to know what's going to happen?"

"But . . ." he started.

I forestalled him. "I'd no' want to know, but to live each day to the fullest like everyone else." I pulled my plaid tight around me. The cold felt as if it had seeped deep inside my bones.

Torquil's face was grave. "Ye've done a bit of growing up, Tor."

I turned away from him and swallowed the lump in my throat, feeling anything but grown.

Torquil retired to a dark corner beneath a length of sail, leaving me to navigate. There was not much in the duty but holding steady and moving ahead. Still the wheel was comforting beneath my fingers and gave me the feel of taking control of my destiny, whatever that might be.

As the clouds drew darker and the day moved on, thoughts of that destiny were not as reassuring as they might have been. I couldn't help but think that I was running away, with little idea as to where I would be safe. It was just like before, but I was alone now and had no friend or mentor to counsel me.

Time passed at a crawl and my fears grew with every league we traveled. My anxiety was such that I felt as if my skin had been flayed raw, and my guts grew more tight and twisted by the moment. Torquil's worry pressed against my mind. Even while he slept, my own became barely manageable.

By the time he woke, late that afternoon, I could hardly wait to give over the wheel. Candle marks of uncertainty had worn me thin. My eyes were as if filled with sand and my head buzzing with bees.

We spoke little as I huddled in my plaid, watching the roll of the waves, drifting between dreams that I could not remember moments after I awoke.

As night drew on we neared the shores of Arbroath. "You don't have to beach it," I said, hefting my pack and looking over the side for rocks below the water's edge. The boat swelled and dipped.

"Just a little closer," he replied. "Best to try and keep yer things dry." He dropped the weight to anchor us. "This is all I can do." He looked torn. "I hate to leave ye like this." I felt the truth of his words and my eyes watered.

He held up his sack of coin. I had left it on the deck where he'd tossed it to me.

I hesitated, then took it. "I'll return it the moment I get back. Give my love to them all."

He rested his hands on my shoulders and pulled me close. "God go with ye, little brother." His voice was rough. I squeezed him back, never wanting to let go, comforted as if my da held me close, as he might never do again. My throat was tight with unshed tears.

"I love ye," I whispered. My face was hot with embarrassment and yet I needed to say the words.

I heard him swallow. When he spoke his voice was gruff. "As do I. Come home again safe, Tormod." I pulled back and he shook me. "I command ye to."

I nodded, hoping and praying that I could.

The boat was knee-high in frigid water, and in moments I could not feel my feet. I waded quickly ashore shaking with cold, quivering with sadness. When I looked back, Torquil was a smudge in the distance.

Be careful. His thoughts brushed the edges of my mind as from a stand of trees, I watched him disappear. Rain fell in fat drops, mixing with the tears slipping down my cheeks. I brushed them away and hurried into my boots. My breeks dripped water and clung to my legs. I had to move inland before it grew too dark to see. Head down, I trudged over the rise and through the woods. The rain came on stronger as my heart felt near to breaking. I had no notion where exactly to find Bertrand and was pleased, when I came upon the village, to see one hut larger than the rest surrounded by grave markers, the usual sign of a kirk. An old well stood at its fore, and as I passed I said a prayer to Our Lady to safeguard my passage.

The Templar and I had been ambushed in a hut that looked much like this one. By the door I lingered, uncertain, equally poised to knock or flee. Then from beyond came the soft cadence of prayer.

I rapped solidly on the old wood and the murmur inside stopped. A moment later a frail, hunched figure appeared. He was a very old man. His hair hung limp and pale around his face, and his eyes were an unnatural milky white. A large wooden crucifix hung on beads around his neck.

"Who is it? Speak." His voice was like the brittle twigs of winter. I shivered.

"I come seeking sanctuary, old Father, an' information if ye will it." The words slid around the chatter of my teeth. As I tipped my head toward him, water dripped from my plaid.

"A lad!" he said with surprise. "Come in. 'Tis no' a night to be out an' about."

"Thank ye, Father. I don't wish to be a burden." The spill of warmth and light beckoned.

"The house o' God is ever open to the faithful," he murmured, gesturing for me to precede him.

It was a good room, if sparsely furnished. Welcoming. A couple of old, thick chairs flanked a wide, squat wooden table, and beside it several woven mats lay among the rushes. Across one wall, an old tapestry was strung, and at the room's center a cook fire burned merrily beneath an old black pot. The scent of its contents wrapped around me like a warm woolen blanket. I took a mat near the fire and held my hands out to chase the chill.

"Ye travel alone, lad?" he asked. "These are no' times of peace and security. Ye should have more o' a care." His blank eyes were turned in my direction.

In the dark of my memory, I saw again those who hunted me. A chill prickled my skin. "Aye. I know that well."

He scooped a thin broth mostly of carrots and potatoes out of the pot into a shallow wooden bowl and handed it to me. "Father, I'm looking for someone said to hail from this village, Bertrand Beaton."

The old man stilled as if I held a poker to his head. "Bertrand? Why are ye lookin' fer Bertrand?" His question was rife with undercurrents. Words whispered at the edges of my mind, but try as I might I could not grasp them.

"We traveled together," I said, not wishing to reveal more and desperately seeking to keep my mind in focus. The room was growing dark and hot. "He invited me to visit."

"Late for a visit," he said suspiciously, then, "but it matters no'. Bertrand is gone from here, lad." My heart dashed at my feet. Not here. What would I do? Where would I go now? My fears were thick in my mind. Panic cut like a million thorns. The room began to fade and my breath grew short.

The old man sensed my distress. "Are ye unwell, lad?" I shook my head, forgetting his lack of sight, then said aloud, "I'll be all right." I took a slow breath, willing my body to make true the statement. "Where, Father? Where has he gone?"

He drew another bowl of soup and sat gingerly. "On sojourn into the Highlands."

The Highlands, I thought, crushed. How was I to find him? I had no skill or experience in tracking.

"Others have been seeking him as well," said the man. My ears pricked and my heart sped. "Soldiers."

"How many? How long ago? What did they ask?" I spit the questions out in a flood.

"Easy, lad. We've time. They've been gone for a fortnight. Bertrand left a week before they arrived," he continued. "Eat an' I'll tell what I can. Ye will need yer strength for the journey ahead." He lifted his bowl.

I watched him sidelong. "Are ye a seer, then?" I asked carefully. The soup sat nearly forgotten in my hands.

"No, just an old man who knows what to expect o' a young man. That ye would go after him is a conclusion foregone." The hut grew quiet and I lifted the bowl to eat.

"There were five," he said. "I canno' see much, so I have no description, but I heard armor and weapons. Their accents were not o' this land." He sipped at the broth. "Bertrand was gone, an' none save myself knew where. I told them nothing." He stared into the fire with blind eyes.

"Do you know where I can find him, then?" I asked, hoping, praying.

"I know the direction an' area. Ye'll have to do a bit o' seek-and-find is my guess, but he's well known in those parts. Ye'll have help." He sat back, his meal done. "There's a ferry in the morning that can take ye up the coast. Eat. Take your rest. Ye're safe here."

The old priest moved to a clear area and lowered himself to his knees. I joined him there and we began to pray. My worry lifted, if only for a while.

A GIFT AND A PRAYER

The morning dawned in far less time than I deemed possible. I slept fitfully and on waking was nearly more tired than when I bedded down. Every few hours I roused from sleep with a cramp in my gut and the remembered dream of soldiers hunting me, yet the smell of hot bannocks and the sight of a porridge pot did much to hearten me. The old priest stooped by the fire, stirring and turning our meal. His hand was braced on his lower back and his legs shook beneath him.

"Here, let me do that," I said, moving quickly to assist him. I stoked the fire and stirred the pot.

"Aye. There's a good lad. These old bones are not as spry as they once were." He rested in one of the chairs as I flipped the oatcakes. Berries dotted the thick batter and the smell was reassuringly like home.

"The ferry will be off within a candle mark. It's on the far side o' the beach through the wood. Shouldn't take ye long to get there. Tell Corbin, the ferryman, Father Angus sent ye an' he'll take care o' ye right and well."

I served him the porridge and one of the bannocks in some ancient tin bowls he had by the fire. His fare was scarce, so I parceled out just enough to take the edge off my hunger and joined him at the table.

"Eat, lad. Take as much as ye can handle. I will be fed here. My people are good. They share what they can an' we all make do." Was he reading my mind? It would not surprise me at this point.

"Where will the ferry take me?" I asked. The bannock was good, the berries tart and juicy. As it turned out, I was hungry and glad that the old priest had urged more on me than I had been willing to take. I'd been fighting nausea since leaving home. It remained in the bottom of my gut, but the hearty fare made it less.

"Stay on till ye reach the shores o' Aberdeen. Then take the road up past Kintore into the high country. Bertrand has gone to the Bruce. The war is gaining momentum, and I fear the need for healers will soon be great."

I turned to ask him if he thought the weather might hold, when suddenly it was as if a spark from the fire had skittered up my inners.

A sail billowed in the breeze. Four squares. Black and white. A white mantle sharp and bright against the dark of day. The hilt of a sword in a sheath that was achingly familiar.

I gasped.

"Lad?" The priest's voice echoed in my ears but my mind was frozen on that single moment in time. The sword . . . What did it mean? I knew that blade. The hilt was distinctive. Who carried the sword of my mentor?

I was surprised and bothered to think that the Order had just passed it to another. Somehow the sword should have stayed with the man or — and how could I ever insist on it — been given to me. I was to be his apprentice.

Surprise gave way to anger. Anger to rage. It washed through me before I knew it was there. My bearings were lost.

I was no longer in the rooms of the kirk, but deep in the midst of a battle. The clang of steel rang in my ears and fury raced in my blood. Men surrounded me on all sides. I reached for my sword, but the scabbard was empty. A man bore down on me and I struck out.

The solid feel of my fist meeting flesh snapped me back to the present. I stared, horrified, at the prone figure of the old priest. He lay amid the rushes, unmoving. The room wavered before my eyes.

What had I done?

"Lord, please allow me the power." The request was purely my heart's cry. Though I didn't deserve it — I had struck an innocent — the lifeblood of the land came to me. Power surged to my fingertips. It was strong, strangely so. My hands were hot and tingling. I dropped at his side, held his head, and closed my eyes. Then with a deep breath, I moved inside.

Beyond bone, blood had begun to pool. I could see it in my mind's eye, and I focused there, feeling the shape and weight of the fine fibers that were his mind.

Though I was unsure of what I was seeing, I did my best to heal the injury. There was, I noticed, an odd pressure in the space behind his eyes, a fluid I was almost sure did not belong. Just to focus the healing there made my insides churn. Unsure, I turned away to try elsewhere, but the power arced from my touch, snaking away, back toward the spot.

Panic rushed through me. I was not skilled in this. The mind was too delicate. I was no healer! Why had I tried?

Then, to my shock, the fluid began to disappear. I came to my senses nearly lying on the man. "Father, forgive me." I scrambled off and helped him to sit. "It comes on sometimes. Truly, I meant ye no harm." I was horrified by what had happened, both before and during my healing. I felt raw and exhausted. My arms felt like weights and there was tightness to my chest. The whole of my world was getting away from me.

"I'm all right, lad. It's no' the worst . . ." His voice dropped off, and suddenly his body grew still. "Lord in Heaven, I can see!" His words were loud in my ears and the room seemed to pulse before me.

"What?" I gasped.

I could do nothing but stare as he hopped about, covering one eye and then the other, shouting out the names of things in the room. He reminded me of the plovers, the tiny birds on the shore that bolted to and fro.

"It's as clear as the day I was born. I've seen naught but shadow for twenty years." His eyes met mine. They were a crystal clear blue. "Ye must have knocked something loose," he said, laughing. "Good for ye, lad. Ye can hit me whenever ye like." The power had healed him.

I smiled, desperately relieved but ill with the way I felt. The power had come to me and I'd used it well. In truth, I could take no credit and I'd most definitely not be hitting him again anytime soon if I had anything to say about it. I said a prayer of thanks to the Lord for granting me this gift and watching over my efforts.

THE STORM

The path was pitted and puddled by rain. I walked along with the feel of his eyes on my back. At the crest of the hill I turned and waved a final farewell, but I was already far away, lost in the memory of the strange visions that had befallen me before I hit the old priest. The hilt of the Templar's sword gleamed before my mind's eye. I had never thought to see it again. The Templar and I had been through much, and that sword had been a part from the very beginning. And what of the other images? This was the second time I'd seen a battle, once in a dream and now in a vision. The same battle? I was not sure. Both the dreams and visions were growing in strength. Before, they had appeared singly, with much time in between. Now they were coming nearly every day and with each my exhaustion deepened. Sleep did nothing to replenish my body. Even now my breath came harshly and I had to stop often to rest.

As I topped the rise, a battered sail flapped in the morning breeze and seabirds circled the ferry swaying in the wash. I hoped the priest would not be charged much for my passage. The barge was ancient, not much more than a flat with rails, a sail, a rudder, and oars.

I moved slowly down the hill, feeling as though I'd walked for leagues, and stood in the wet grass, waiting as the ferryman prepared to push off. Midges swarmed my head and I slapped at them impatiently.

"Father Angus said you would take me where I need," I said. He looked me over sharply and I began to sweat. Did he know I was hunted?

"Aye, then, very well. Come along. I owe the good Father much."

The ferryman was near on the age of my da and his body was just as strong. His skin held many leathered creases and was deeply brown from the sun. I hefted my pack and gingerly climbed aboard.

"Don't get many single travelers hereabout. Where are ye bound?" he asked, shoving off with a pole.

"Aberdeen," I said. Father Angus gave me directions by land to Kintore. Bertrand had been headed there.

"Got family thereabouts, d'ye?" he asked, adjusting the oars.

"Mmm," I mumbled, nodding. I didn't encourage more conversation between us. I could feel the man's curiosity, and it was playing havoc with my ability to control myself from blurting out the answers he sought. Looking for relief, I focused on a twist of clouds that swirled against the darkening sky.

I shivered in my plaid. The temperature had dropped overnight, and it was still not quite dry all the way through. The ferryman set to rowing and left me to my thoughts. *Where were the men seeking me? If soldiers had been through here weeks ago, were they the same ones that had boarded Da's boat? Or were there more? And where had they gone?* I had no faith that I had turned them permanently away. My push had been weak.

My body was tight and my mouth, inordinately dry. As we moved slowly up the coast, I eyed the rough water with a strong sense of unease. Each pull of the oars brought the sea rushing over the outer frame of the boat. "What's happening?" I asked.

"Bit o' a squall blowin' up. Odd, though. I didn't see it coming." As he spoke, waves crashed our edges. A wind off the port side cut and whipped the sail. "I've got to take us beyond the next inlet. It's closer to the land

and sheltered from the wind. Grab hold o' the mast. This is a devil." He cursed and struggled with the oars.

Twisted and anxious, I watched for the shore. *Odd, though. I didn't see it coming.* The man's words reverberated in my mind. And then I knew.

This was not a normal storm. The water was too violent, the wind biting too hard. I had something to do with it. My worry had brought the storm.

Beneath my breath I began the prayer of Our Lord, begging Him to still the wind. The waves became deeper, and the boat rocked perilously. "Please," I said aloud.

"I'm doin' all I can." The ferryman was white. He dug in hard and moved us slowly.

"Please," I whispered desperately, fighting not to lose my guts. I closed my eyes tightly and at once a brilliant glow filled the space behind my lids. Through the brightness came the image of the carving and bowl. A flare of power suddenly flooded my body, sliding along my skin, heating my blood and filling me with joy. I threw my arms wide and opened my eyes to the heavens and, all at once, the ocean calmed. The wind followed moments later and the air temperature rose.

"Lord have mercy," I heard the ferryman exclaim. He dropped to his knees and crossed himself.

It was then I realized how strange I must have looked. Quickly, I lowered my arms and averted my eyes.

Moving to the far side of the platform, I hunched in my plaid, drawing it up over my head. I dropped down against the frame and covertly watched the ferryman, trying desperately not to feel his fear or hear the whisper of his thoughts. He took us back to open sea, but was not at all happy to do it. The sail filled as if there had never been a problem, and we pressed forward once again. I closed my eyes and thought longingly of the Holy Vessel.

The man did not speak to me again as we drifted up the coast, but I heard his thoughts and they were not comforting. Passengers joined us at stops along the way, and I thanked the Lord for sending them. The ferryman's fear pressed against me so strongly, I felt it as if it were my own. My senses became muddled, and I found myself jumping at every sound or sudden movement and having thoughts that made me quake with terror. *Soldiers are looking for Bertrand. They were at the preceptory. They knew about me. They could be anywhere. At any landing, they might lie in wait. Trapped. I would be trapped and all o' this would be over.*

The air grew colder as the day wore on and the damp that hung over the ocean seeped into my skin. Even with a blanket atop my plaid, my body shook. Deep inside, my bones ached. I was hot, then cold, and my nose dripped no matter how many times I dried it with my sleeve. I tried to sleep, but could only achieve fits and starts of dark dreaming. Men in shadows. The rustle of armor. Voices. *"Find him. Bring him to me."*

My body leapt, jolted awake by the sound of an argument. A family had gotten on, and two of the young ones were having a row. It was so like the bairns at home my eyes filled with tears. Cold, wet, tired, and ill, I wanted nothing more than to be with my family.

My thoughts raced as fragments of memories spilled across the surface of my mind. Past. Present. The old lives that the Holy Vessel had shown to me; flashes of the Protectors that had come before. My skin was slick with perspiration, and it felt as if a fever rushed through my veins. Emotions flit. Fear. Anger. Loneliness. Confusion.

The family with the feuding bairns was closer to me now. The da was trying to keep the lads from one another while their mam held a wee lass curled up in her lap. Her worry over their journey hit me at once and whispers of thought enveloped my mind.

I could not still my sudden shaking as the thoughts of not only her, but other passengers started slipping through my shielding. I had to shut them out, but I couldn't seem to rouse myself to it.

"Am I mistaken, or does that lad look a bit unwell?" said the mother.

"Should we move to the other side o' the platform?" asked the father. "He is white in the gills. Illness o' the sea, most like. Lad, what's wrong with ye? Ferryman, I don't like the look o' this."

"Hush ye now, Luke. It's no' his fault if he's feeling poorly," the woman's voice said. I felt burning hot, where moments ago I'd been cold. The ferryman put out the oars, grumbling, then crouched before me, barking out questions for which I had no answers.

I closed my eyes just for a moment, drifting, but woke as the ferry grounded ashore. Beneath my arms I felt the grip of hands, holding, lifting, and moving me. I wanted to push him away, to shout at him to put me down, but I couldn't make my body work. It was as if I was locked away behind a wall so thick it could not be breached. The man slung me over his back, and I felt a cold rush of water on my feet as he waded ashore, and then dropped me hard on the beach. I hurt all over. *Where is he going?* I heard the thud of my sack landing in the sand beside me.

"Here now! Ye canno' just leave him there," the woman from the ferry exclaimed. "He's a lad, an' he's ill."

"This is his stop, an' I'm no' his keeper. He'll make his way. People are waiting farther on," said the ferryman.

No! Don't leave me here. There's something wrong. I canno' move. Deep in my mind I was screaming, but the words would not move past my lips. I heard the swish of his oars as they beat the waves.

"Ye're heartless. Ye leave him to die!" The mother's angry words floated across the sea.

"Feel free to get out with him, then," the ferryman snapped without pausing in his pull of the oars.

"I canno'. We've got to make it to Banff tonight." Her worry for me warred with her concern for her family.

And then they were gone.

UNLIKELY SAVIOR

Sand blew over me as I lay on my side, curled up in a ball. Cold seeped into my body, past the blanket and plaid. There was no beginning, no end to the shudders that wracked me. My teeth chattered furiously. Visions crashed over me, ever changing bits and pieces.

"What do you mean they demand surety? I am the King of France!"

"With all humble acknowledgment, sire, you do owe a debt that is beyond sizable. Payment to the Templars are far in arrears." The voice was silken, cunning.

"*The Templars,*" the King spat, "*have more wealth than any single body in the world! Whatever we owe them is nothing in comparison. Let them wait!*"

"*Sire, ye need more money from them, and they will not send it otherwise. Our armies need to be paid, else they find employment on other sides. It is not so great a thing they ask.*"

Rage filled the space in my mind and I nearly passed into the black.

"*Not so great! They demand the crown jewels! The very symbol of Kingship!*"

"*Just for safekeeping, sire. Just until the monies come from the campaign abroad. It will do no harm. They will be safer in the guarded vaults of the Templars than anywhere else.*"

"Here, boy? What the devil is wrong?" The voice pierced my vision and as hands grasped my arms and turned me roughly, I could suddenly move and speak again.

"Cold," I said, shaking.

"Yes, ye are cold. Why wouldn't ye be? Ye're layin' about in the wet sand. Can ye sit? I'll help."

It was a lass, near on my age. Her hair was a deep red, much darker than my carrot orange, and it was a snaking mass of curls that covered her face as she leaned over me.

"Aye," I rasped, chattering.

"Ye're burning up," she said, laying the cool backs of her hands on my face. "Ye'd best be getting along home now. Rain is about to fall and yer already ailin'." She spoke quickly with an accent a bit different from my own.

"Canno'. No home," I managed through teeth that would not stop clacking together. I was having trouble focusing on the shape of her. Dark and light were fading one to the next.

"No home!" she exclaimed. "How did ye come to be here? Where d'ye think yer going? Why the devil are ye just sitting there no' answering me?" The short and rapid questions were making my head spin. It was not only the questions she spoke but also the ones she thought. Her feelings and energy were tearing me apart.

"Stop," I bellowed. "How in Hades can I answer ye, with all that blatherin'? God's toes, lass, yer like a fish-wife." I held my head as it pounded, but my outburst seemed to draw me out of the strange haze that had wrapped around me. It did nothing, though, for my twisting and churning guts.

She stopped and stared at me, and for the first time I saw her face. It was as pale as the first light of morning, sprinkled with a shine of cinnamon freckles. Her eyes were a brilliant blue and at this moment they crackled with pure venom.

"Blatherin' is it?" I had no warning at all to prepare myself. She drew back and hit me square in the eye.

Pain shot through my head as if a white-hot poker had been shoved there. In the space of a heartbeat I was laid out flat on the sand again. Above me she stood, fists curled and ready to black my other eye.

I couldn't believe it. "Yer daft as well," I shouted, gripping my head and moaning. *Lord, why? What is wrong with her?*

"Watch it, man. Yer troubling my conscience as it is. I'd hate to have to hide ye again, since yer obviously not up to it." She stood over me with clenched fists.

I curled on my side, willing her, the pain, and the misery away. "Maybe ye could just leave me to die?" I suggested, knowing she wouldn't, half hoping she would.

"I surely ought to," she said, plopping down. I felt her presence close by.

The shaking began then, soft rolls rippling from head to toe. I couldn't tell if it was from pain or cold. I felt both in abundance.

"Damnation," she muttered, sounding as if she were eyeing me like a piece of rotten meat. "Come on. Ye can't stay here. But, I warn ye, man, the folk that board me, my uncle and his wife, will not be takin' ye in as well.

It's with the cows ye'll have to hide. Just a byre, but it's a sure sight better than here."

As she spoke, the horizon began to tilt and all of the colors around me faded. She grabbed my arm and hauled me upright and, strangely, the darkness slid away and I was able to think. The vision. The French King. Something about the Templars and the crown jewels.

"Ye're no' from these parts. That's as clear as the morning sky. Where are ye coming from? Where are ye bound?" Her words tumbled over one another and her movements were quick and sure. She dropped my arm and popped to her feet, and the world tilted again with a frenzied wash of dizziness.

"Please," I begged, "just take me to the cows." I pulled my plaid tight around me. It did nothing to still the shaking or stop my head from pounding. "I'll be off again in the morning and trouble ye no more." I squinted up at her. Even the low light of the day was too bright for my eyes.

"Lord and Lady, ye really are in a bad way, aren't ye?" she exclaimed. She took my arm more gently this time and I was amazed. The headache, the nausea, and the shivers somehow dulled when she touched me. I stared, my mouth agape.

"Who are ye?" I mumbled. *And how can yer touch settle me this way?* I thought.

"Aine Cleary," she replied.

I was so surprised by the relief I felt when she touched me, that I didn't move fast enough. Her arm slid from mine and the misery returned with a fury.

"Please," I whispered, fighting off the faint, reaching for her hand.

She misunderstood. "Hang on, now. I'll help." She took both of my palms in hers and tugged until I was on my feet. The wind cut across the shore and, weak, I swayed and leaned into her body.

She gasped. "Here now! Don't ye be taking liberties with me, man. I'm here to help ye, but I'll knock ye flat again, if I think there's even a bit of improper behavior."

She *was* daft. Improper behavior? I could barely keep the bile that rose in my throat from spilling. Still, I knew that touching her was somehow making survival a slight possibility, so I let her rant. As for laying me out, it was a good thing my da made it clear that I couldn't thump lasses.

As we struggled up and over the rise, I pushed away thoughts of revenge and concentrated on making it to a shelter where I could lie down and die. The woods were dark and wet. Mounds of leaves tangled around my feet as I stumbled along, trying to keep pace so that she wouldn't let go. I didn't know what to make of the strange response I was having toward her.

We came to the byre in a time almost faster than I wanted, knowing she could not forever hold on to me. It was three stone walls and a sloped thatched roof held up by thick wooden beams. A rickety half gate closed off the entrance. It was not home, but I was just as glad to see it. Even with her help the short walk had stolen nearly all my strength.

There were five cows, two sheep, and several horses milling and murmuring in the dark, dank space. "Move it now, Gracious, or I'll no' be bringing in yer milk in the morning," Aine said, pushing our way through the warm bodies. "Aye, Forlorn, that's a good girl. Shove along, dearlin'."

"Odd names for animals," I mumbled.

"Aye, well, they're not their real names, o' course, but I think they suit better, an' they're like friends this way. Gracious is always the last to eat, like she's being polite. An' that one, Forlorn, seems sad, somehow." She helped me to a pile of hay in an open corner.

"An' the others?" I asked, just to keep her talking and close by my side. She let go to stretch, and the illness came on again like the fierce blow of winter. I turned to my side and pulled my cloak tight. Hurt. My head. My body.

"Well, there's Pernicious, an' Suspicious, an' Jordy . . ." Her voice sounded far off. Like perhaps I was beneath the water. "Ye don't look good. Don't ye go dying on me. It'll bring a mess o' trouble."

I couldn't answer. I was concentrating on breathing and trying not to lose the small contents of my stomach. It was nearly more than I could manage.

"Aine!" A woman's shrill voice broke through the quiet of my misery.

She hurried toward the gate. "I'm going now. Please. Don't die." She seemed to hesitate. "I don't have many friends here aside from the cows," she said, nearly to herself.

"Aine! Where the devil are ye, girl?" The voice was much closer this time.

"I'll be back as soon as I can," she said, and disappeared.

INTO THE DARKNESS

Pain was my every thought and movement. It was as if my heartbeat pumped the aching pulse into my head and spread it like flames throughout my body. I shook, whole body tremors, while darkness claimed and spit me back out again like the pit of a cherry. Dreams filled the blackness. Some were so real and terrifying that I doubted where the waking began and the sleeping ended.

"*Confess!*" Smoke. Flames. "*Tell me where the false God's idol is hidden!*"

"*I will no'!*"

"*Then you will die and your Holy Brethren will be brought to the ground.*"

Fire. Jeering crowds. A white mantle. Smoke.

I thrashed, jolting awake. It was dark and I hurt all over. "Where am I? Can anyone hear me?" The hum of a tune pricked at my ears. I reached for the sound and peace stole over me. *Sleep,* it whispered. And I did.

When I woke it was with the knowledge that she sat beside me. "What happened?" I whispered. My lips were cracked and they burned when I spoke. A rustle of movement played in my ears, and I opened my eyes a slit. It took some time for anything to take shape in the dimness.

"Ye've been ill," she said as she unfolded her thin legs from beneath her. She had been tucked up in a ball beside me. I felt her exhaustion. The bristling edginess she had shown me before was now gone. She seemed uncertain, shy. "What's yer name?" she asked, a yawn escaping.

"Tormod," I said, barely rousing the energy to speak. "Water?" My voice felt strange in my throat and my thoughts were a jumble. The skin on my body felt tight near bursting and I was hot all over.

"Aye. Here." She held a skin to my lips and a warm, brackish trickle slid down my throat.

"How long?" I asked, struggling to put days together in my mind and words in my mouth.

"Ye've been in and out since yesterday." Her voice was as rusted as mine.

"Ye sang to me," I said, seeking her eyes in the darkness. Her face was near, but she averted her eyes and shrugged. I saw the bare movement of it ruffle her hair. "Aye. It seemed to give ye peace." Her voice was not much more than a whisper.

"It helped, I think," I said.

She said nothing more.

"I need to . . ." I trailed off, uneasy. I had to void, badly.

She stared at me, her blue eyes glowing. I waited for it to register, and then a flush of embarrassment slid through her to me. It was hard to see, but I thought perhaps her face was red.

"Oh, aye." She scrambled to her feet and took my hand. This time there was little change inside me. She helped me up. My legs felt weak, and I was hungry.

"Hold the beam here. I will make sure no one's about. William took off at first light, but he might be back by now." I had no idea who William was, and had little desire to ask.

She crept quietly outside and a moment later waved me forward. My body rippled with chill. Slipping over the wet ground, I began to climb behind the lean-to. "Here," she said, handing me an old cloth rag.

I nodded and went about my business. It must have been raining the whole time I'd been out of my senses, for the puddles were deep and the wood was drenched.

She was waiting for me when I came around the front, and she followed me back inside. Her eyes were enormous and wary.

"What?" I asked. "Why d'ye look at me that way? Last I recall, ye wanted to knock me flat." I wouldn't normally have drawn attention to the idea that I'd received a thrashing at the hands of a lass, but she seemed to need to be put at ease. I felt her disquiet ripple between us.

"Ye . . ." She hesitated. "Did things when ye were out o' yer head. D'ye no' remember?" Her face was pink and her hands were nervously grasping her sark, pleating the material over and over again.

Immediately, I was frightened. Had I harmed her in any way? She didn't seem different, but I had a vague memory of her arms around me. "If I acted badly, I can assure ye that I'm truly sorry," I said. It was uncomfortable not to know something I might have done, as if a part of my mind and memory could not be trusted.

The flush of pink became an angry red and her eyes returned to their crackling blue, telling me that she was readying a fist. I had the image again of her hands on my forehead. "Ye'd be sorry, would ye?" she said. "What now, am I no' good enough for the likes o' ye?" The bristle of anger lashed out at my mind and nearly toppled me. What had I said? Beneath her anger was hurt. I struggled to establish when I might have offended her.

"I only meant that I was no' in my right mind." Her fist curled and tightened. "I mean, I barely know ye. I've more manners than to . . ." I hesitated, searching for a word that would not be uncomely. ". . . make advances toward a lass I don't know." Now I was flushed. Embarrassment swirled about my mind, cramping my body, but I felt her relax. "If that's not what ye meant, what then?" I asked.

It was her turn to stumble through the words. "Well, ye . . ." she mumbled, then cleared her throat. "An' I don't know how ye did it, mind ye, but whenever ye were dreaming . . ." She seemed truly discomforted.

"Aye," I encouraged.

"I knew yer dreams," she said quickly.

I gaped at her.

68

"Go on, think me mad, but I was there. There's no other way I can tell it to ye. I saw things that I couldn't make up if I tried. Believe it or don't. It's nothing to me one way or another."

Her bravado was false. Nervousness rolled off her in waves. The thing was, I did believe her, but it frightened the life out of me. "What did ye see?" I asked.

"I saw a road atop a great mountain," she said with awe. "An' a horse that fell an' screamed. It broke my heart."

Gooseflesh slid over me. Yes, she knew my dreams, well and truly.

"Listen to me. What ye saw was naught but a dream. Ye must never speak o' it." My eyes held hers with urgency.

"But how did ye do it?" she asked.

I wanted no more of this conversation. "Never."

"Aine." A man's deep voice sounded from outside the lean-to, so close she leapt from me.

"Hide." She shoved me back into the corner. "Quick with ye, man. Under the hay," she whispered urgently. "Do it now!"

A PAINFUL JUSTICE

I dove beneath a thick pile of straw. It was not fresh, and she shoveled more of the same over me before I could argue. The gate squealed and thumped. Light overtook the darkness and my eyes began to swim. "Ye should have been done with this a long time ago," I heard him say.

Anger pressed against the edges of my mind. Aine didn't speak. She had moved away from me to the opposite corner and I could feel her blind terror.

"Stupid, lazy girl." His mean words hung in the empty air. "Waste o' food, ye are." He was moving toward her. "What, no smart words from ye?" The hairs on my neck bristled. As he advanced on her, she backed away. The muck shovel hung limp in her hands.

Fear lashed out at me suddenly, a terror so deep it stole my breath.

"I've told ye before haven't I, Aine?" He reached out and squeezed her arm. I could see the white spots where his fingers pressed tightly. I felt the scream rising within her.

Everything in me tensed, and I felt the power calling

out to me. I shouldn't do it. It was dangerous, and I was weak.

His jaw tightened and flexed as he shook her. "Ye know well the punishment for disobeying me, don't ye?" She only stared at him with wide eyes. There was nothing I could do but push. *She's nothing to ye. Beneath yer notice.* Pain rocked my head, and the push had no effect. My resources were too low. He grabbed hold of her hair and Aine's panic howled in my mind. Her fear and my own smashed into each other and grew. My head pounded as sweat poured from my body. Still, I pushed.

I felt the pulse swell between my ears, and my head felt near bursting, the pressure was so high. *Yer wife will see the bruises.* Push. A flash of his memories slid through me. My ears were ringing. *She knows where ye buried the last servant girl's body.* Push. Bile rose high and thick, choking me. Push.

He finally thrust her forcefully aside, his eyes wild and darting around the place. The beat of his heart was erratic. I could feel it in my chest. *She'll tell.* His vile thoughts filled my head. *Dirty, lying girl. Must stop her from opening her rotten, telling lips.*

My heart dropped. I couldn't breathe. No! This was not supposed to happen. Wait!

His meaty fist rose in the air, and the muscles in his forearm clenched.

Pure, raw power streamed to my call. It poured through my entire being. As his fist started down, I focused the power directly into his mind. Everything I had seen, all I had been through — the hurt, the pain, and the loss — fueled my attack. And it was an attack, there was no mistaking that. I wanted him dead, for what he'd done and what he intended to do.

The man's body jerked, as if unseen hands gripped and shook him hard. His eyes grew wide and terrified and rolled back in his head. Spittle gurgled from his lips and he crumbled to the earthen floor.

"No, Tormod. Stop!" But the power would not be contained. It surged in waves without end. Flowing. Crashing. Burning.

Focus! The command snapped so loud in my ears that it shook me into action. I quickly emptied my mind of everything but the desire to stop. It was so sudden I nearly forgot what came next.

Ground. The second command seemed to material-ize inside my head, and the earth was solid and strong beneath me, the wind outside whipping hard. Aine's hands found me through the hay and, once again, her presence made the difference.

"Shield," I said aloud.

The power dropped away and slid back into the earth from whence it had come. Only fear, panic, and guilt remained. Dear Lord, what had I done? My breath rasped in the darkness. A dead man lay before me. I had killed again, and this time on purpose. Guilt crowded my heart and tears filled my eyes as I weakly crawled away from the body. I had no right. I had no control. I knew that long before arriving here. "Why? Why did I try? I am a beast." I didn't realize the words I spoke were aloud.

"No." Aine's whisper was strong. I couldn't look at her. "Tormod." Her fingers forced my face to hers. "He was an abomination." She could barely form the words. "I had nowhere to run. No one would have believed me. I don't know how ye did it, but ye saved me."

I tried to embrace what she'd said, to accept that what I'd done was worth the price on my soul, but I could not reconcile it. I shook my head, trying to clear it. I was so ill, so very twisted inside that I could barely move.

"Tormod. Stay with me. We have to be gone from here. Please!" With her hands on my arms I managed to get to my feet. "It won't be long till they find him. Ye'll be hung. We've got to go!" In the dimness her face was pale.

"We?" I gasped.

"Aye," she replied. "I canno' stay here. I've nowhere to go." She was not asking. "I'm coming with ye." Her voice was loud, demanding. I didn't know what to do. It was one thing to run by myself, but to be responsible for the life of another . . . ? I was trying to think, but my head was foggy and my body battered by the power use. I truly didn't think I could go on without her. "Aye. Together," I said quickly.

We crept outside, leading one of the horses. Though we needed to hurry, my movements were slow and awkward and the sudden brightness nearly took me low. Mist hovered around our feet and my breath floated on the cool air. Beneath the gray of the morning sky, a pale yellow sun was emerging.

"Hurry! The horse is strong. We can ride together. I'll help." I was struggling to make my body work, to heed her urgency. The saddle was high, and it took much from both of us to get me astride. Aine scrambled nimbly into place behind me and the moment our legs touched and she settled against my back the world calmed.

"Aine? Where are ye, ye lazy girl? The cows are fair set to bursting." The woman's muttering was near. I could feel her approach. I gave the horse his head and kneed him on. We were across the field when her shrill cry cut the air.

"William!" Her pain cut through the barrier Aine was providing, and I nearly fell from the horse.

As we sped over the rise and out of her sight, I hunched low and reached for the mind of our horse. He took on speed and the village disappeared behind us. Aine was wrapped tightly around me. It was then that I was hit with the inevitable exertion, and my eyes grew dim. I felt Aine's arms tighten and her hands close over mine on the reins. It was all I could do to fight the blackness reaching for me.

FUGITIVES

We rode north and west, though I was barely aware of it. Aine kept me upright and pushed the horse to make distance. We stuck to the main road and followed its twisting, rutted path deep into the heart of Highland country. The going was rough and our speed erratic. Rain began again midmorning, light, misty, and cold. We were soaked through in little time and spoke not at all.

Aine clung to my back. I could feel her shivering. As the shock and fear of what I had done played in her thoughts and pressed against my mind, it built the wall of guilt and regret so high in me that by midday I was lying against the horse's neck in nearly a faint.

Aine slowed and stopped the horse as we came to an overhang of ledge, deep in a forested vale. "We'll not find a better place to rest," she said. I slid down from the saddle and landed shakily. I lost contact with her for the first time since morning.

It was as if the air was sucked from my lungs. The pulse of the land and the whisper of the trees crashed and pounded loud in my ears. All of my fears spiraled and became entangled with hers. I cried out as my body began to shake and, in response, Aine's fear grew yet again. The forest began to fade.

And then from the darkness, a thread of sound broke through. Aine's song surrounded me, filling the clearing, and the world went still. The horrible press of feeling was blessedly silenced and my mind was fixed on the strange and haunting melody. It had no beginning or end, no pattern that could be anticipated. I felt the power rise up out of the land and engulf us, and within my mind a perfect harmony settled. The chaos stilled and I could once again breathe.

"What was that?!" I gasped as the song faded and her faraway gaze sharpened.

"I don't know what ye're talking about," she muttered, turning away.

I was confused. Had she done something? Before I could ask, her body wavered and I reached for her. As my hands touched her shoulders, I was flooded with images. *A family stricken, bairns too ill to lift their heads, pleading, begging with their eyes. Aine sitting among them singing and crying.*

Her family? I pushed away the memories as if scalded. To read these thoughts uninvited was surely a trespass. I dropped my hands and moved a pace away. She hunched down on herself.

What was I to make of this? Was it her? Was it me?

"Lord, it's cold," she mumbled. Her body was shaking.

I had the plaid tight about me. She had only her sark. I peeled off the woolen and offered it to her.

"Thank ye, Tormod," she said.

"I forgot what it's like to travel in the rain," I said. She seemed to need me to stop talking about what had happened, so I did. Aine moved off in search of wood beneath the overhang.

"It's been wet awhile, but maybe we can manage a fire with bits from the back," I said. She rubbed her hands briskly together, trying no doubt to get warm.

"I'll take the rain an' a new life over the one I left," she said softly as she rooted for wood. "Is there anything we can use for tinder?" She seemed determined to put the incident behind.

I moved sluggishly to find sticks and leaves that had escaped the rain. My body was tired, down to the ends of my fingers and toes. I fumbled the flint from my pack and Aine moved on to feed and water the horse. She could deny that she had done anything, but I could feel the exhaustion and sadness billowing from her. It surrounded and squeezed me. She was feeling poorly and it was from using the power. I was sure of it. And though her singing had somehow helped strengthen my shielding, I could feel it once again begin to thin. Her mood was becoming mine.

I stumbled to the small pile of wood and twigs and set spark to the tinder. It was smoky and slow and I gave up after a time. Instead I fished an apple and some dried herring from the pack. "Best I can do," I said, offering both to Aine.

She took the apple. I waved toward the pack. "There's more in the sack. Help yerself to whatever ye want."

"This is good for now. I'm not so much hungry as tired." She ate without relish and moved to the back of the shelter and slumped down. I joined her there. The patter of rain from beyond pulled me toward sleep. I could not sense any of her thoughts and was glad of it. When she closed her eyes a slow trickle of tears leaked from their edges. She pulled the plaid closer to hide them.

I hated when lasses cried. It twisted something deep inside and made me sad and uncomfortable. She didn't invite me to talk about it, which was all right. Just feeling what she did made me want to cry as well. Instead I gave in to sleep.

GIFTS UNCOVERED

I woke cold, damp, and cramped from head to toe, but at least the rain had stopped. Aine's head lay against my shoulder and with some slow shifting I found I could study her face. She was pretty when she wasn't railing at me or crying, I decided. Her hair had a kind of red-gold glow that hung in a tangle of curls. Her skin was pale, but light freckles covered much of it.

Aine stirred and opened her eyes, and I felt as if I had been caught doing something wrong. Heat colored my cheeks. Her feelings were, thankfully, no longer pressing their way into my mind. But as I couldn't read her, I was surprised when she asked, "What did ye do to William?"

What should I do? Deny that I'd done anything or try to explain it? "I don't really know. He made me sore angry."

Her gaze sharpened. "Aye. I get angry as well, but my thoughts are no' enough to kill a man." She sat up, breaking contact, and I felt both her fear and the determination she had to overcome it.

"Well, I'm not so much like ye." I rested my head on my arms and stared at her. "I'm different." It was all

I could say. How could I possibly explain any of this to her?

"We're more alike than ye might credit. I am different as well," she said softly. Her bright blue gaze held mine steadily and I could not look away.

"Want to tell me about it?" I asked. My heart was beating strongly in my chest. I was taking a chance. Asking her to trust me.

"Tell me about ye, first," she said.

Trust asking for trust. I paused. She knew already something about the man's death and my involvement. Her gaze was open and honest. I took a deep breath. "I have strange abilities. I can do things no other can," I said.

She nodded and the fear crackling beneath the surface of her seemed to settle. "As can I." Her voice was almost too soft to hear. "What did ye do to William?"

How could I explain it to her? "I convinced him that there were other things more important than hurting ye."

"Aside from the how of it, he believed ye?"

"No. No' at first." The conversation was beginning to make me uncomfortable.

"How did ye convince him?" she persisted.

I didn't realize opening up to her would really mean telling her the whole truth. "It doesn't matter. I had to make him stop. He was hurting ye." I wanted her to drop it. This was a mistake.

"Tormod, how did ye convince him? Please, tell me." She would not leave it alone. Sweat was rising on my skin and I was growing agitated.

"Tormod!"

"He killed another girl, Aine! I convinced him ye knew where the body was." There, I'd said it. Now maybe she would stop pestering.

"Ye saw his memories." Her hand went to her mouth, and she whispered the words as if they frightened her more than anything.

I nodded.

"I did as well," she said. "I knew what he'd done. It was there, in the barn. I can see things that have happened in the recent past," she said. Her own words seemed to stun her.

My mouth dropped and I gaped at her, shocked. I don't know what I expected. Something about the singing, perhaps, but this ability was akin to my own.

The shock on my face set off her ire. "What? Ye don't think a lass could be like ye?"

That was nearly exactly what I had been thinking. Could she read my mind? I was suddenly uneasy. "I just never knew any," I said truthfully. "I thought ye'd speak o' the singing. Ye surprised me."

"I do that as well. It's this other thing that stands out more, though."

"How d'ye mean ye see what's past?"

"When I come on a place, I can sometimes tell who has been to it recently or something that has happened there. It's like an echo." She was quiet, somber then. "I wish that I had known how to kill him."

"No! Ye don't. It's terrible to bear the death of another, Aine. No matter what he did, he was a man an' I took his life. I had no right," I said.

A wash of sadness rolled through her, then on to me. "What is it?" I asked.

"I've killed as well, Tormod. An' it was people who did no' deserve to die." She wouldn't meet my eye. She did not speak for a long moment, and I concentrated on the drip of the rain and the shift and sway of the trees. I let the pulse of the forest's life calm me. Her voice was so soft and low that when she began again, I had to fight to hear. "I killed them, Tormod. My family is gone an' it's my fault."

I was confused. I knew her memories even if she was unaware of it. Her family had died of illness. "Ye didn't, Aine. I saw what happened. Illness took yer family. Ye canno' take responsibility for that."

She shook her head. "I begged them to go to market, Tormod. We didn't go every year, an' we weren't set to yet. I talked them into it. An' on the way we passed through a village whose memories lay strong enough for me to see."

Her hands were wringing the plaid and her face was pale with the remembering. "I read the place. I saw the illness, but I was caught up in wanting to get to market an' I didn't heed the signs. I didn't tell anyone. They never knew." She choked on the last.

"There was naught ye could have done about it, lass. I know what yer feeling. I've faced like situations. It's no' yer fault, ye didn't recognize the danger. An' truly, could ye have told them? Would they have listened?"

She took a deep breath. "Yer the first one I've ever talked to about it, the first who might understand. No. I guess they wouldn't have believed me even if I insisted." She rolled over and sat up. "It doesn't make me feel any better. I lived an' they died."

I didn't argue. I felt as she did and it got me nowhere. We had both survived when others hadn't. I didn't know why any more than she did.

"So ye too can read the past o' a place?" she asked.

"Not like I think ye can. I have visions, bits an' pieces of both the past an' the future come to me, but they're never complete. I only see a little at a time, like I'm looking through a hole."

She nodded. "I see it all an' I'd much rather no' most times. It's rare strange to speak about it at all." She paused, in thought. Then she stood and offered me a hand up. "I'm starving. An' stayin' here is no' an option. Let's eat and go."

I nodded and accepted her hand. A gentle hum of vibration slid through me all the way to my shields when my fingers touched hers. I didn't know what to make of, or do, about it.

She misinterpreted my quiet. "Are ye feelin' badly?"

"No. I am fairly well just now." The horse was grazing beyond the overhang and I took a long drink of water from the skin. Aine drew two apples from the pack and gave me one.

"So, where *are* we goin'?" she asked.

"To seek a healer o' our kind, Bertrand Beaton by name." I stood and tied my pack to the saddle, then climbed astride and offered her a hand up.

"There are more? Like us, I mean?" she asked. The surprise in her voice was familiar. I had been just as shocked by the notion when it was first suggested to me.

"Aye. From what I'm told, there are many. I was supposed to apprentice with them." I could feel her curiosity peak.

"Ye were to be a healer's apprentice?" she asked.

"A Templar's apprentice," I replied. Even now the words felt good on my tongue, and the look of wonder that passed over her features pleased me.

"I would give anything to be one!" she exclaimed.

"You? A lass?" A sharp laugh escaped before I could rein it in.

Her legs firmed on the ground and with a strong jerk on my arm she toppled me off the horse before I knew what happened. My aching body hit the dirt and I rolled away from the horse's hooves with great effort.

"Are ye daft?!" I shouted. "Damnation! Do that again and ye'll be sorrier than ye can ever imagine." Fury rose and rippled through me like the strike of lightning. "Ye know well that it could never be," I snapped, at the same time confused and frightened by the intensity of the feelings rushing over me. It made my head spin. Slowly I crawled to my feet, trying to reorient myself. "It's an order of monks. They're no' even allowed in the presence of women. Can ye imagine for one moment that they would accept one as a member?"

She had the grace to look away even though I could feel her seething. I climbed back into the saddle, not at all helpful to her as she worked to get up behind me.

"It's nothing against ye personally," I grumbled. "From what I've seen, ye'd give them a devil o' a hard time." I said the last beneath my breath, but she heard nonetheless, and I felt a ripple of amusement slide from her to me. Placidly she wrapped her arms around my waist. I wanted to throw them off to spite her, but my body and mind had already begun to settle with the contact and my anger grew less. I urged the horse on without another word.

UNLEASHED

We followed the sun as it worked its way across the land, skirting as many of the crofts as we were able. There were, no doubt, even more factions hunting me now. It was frightening to know that now I had more enemies than friends. News did not generally travel fast but word of murder was sure to reach the watch, the Highland group of men who kept the law. It would not be safe to test our luck at any of the homesteads within days of Aine's former home.

Aine tried at conversation several times, but I didn't encourage her. It was not the falling out of the morning, but a growing sense of general unease that hovered. By late afternoon I felt the chaos rising within me, and even her touch did not bank the fire. It was growing more and more difficult to sit upright. Every once in a while, she hummed in my ear and the feelings settled enough for me to bear, but it was never for very long.

Just before sundown we stopped in a grove beside a

rushing burn to rest. We ate some carrots and cheese that the old Father had sent along, but the food lay hard in my stomach. Aine saw to the horse and then sat down near me and began once more to softly sing. The worst of my queasiness evened out.

"D'ye know how far away the village is?" She was tired. I could see it in her face. Darkness bruised the space above her cheeks.

"It can't be far now," I said with a confidence I didn't feel. Just then a gust of wind lifted the bare branches around us, and fear tore through my mind. Aine stilled and a wash of emotion surged from her to me.

"Someone approaches." I leapt to my feet and drew my dagger, quickly stepping in front of her. "We travel to our uncle's in Straloch. You are my sister," I said urgently.

She nodded and we waited for their arrival. The sound of the horse's hooves was loud in my ears. I concentrated on the feel of them. It was a ragtag group. Hungry. Petty. Dangerous. At the back of my mind, Aine's low hum sounded. I latched on to it to calm myself as I scanned the level of power beneath the ground and among the trees. The slow and steady thrum of life was comforting. Full to bursting and tempting me to call upon it.

"What do we have here? Two wee cockerels ripe for the pickin'?" The man was skin and bones, and he smelled as if he had never come in contact with water or lye soap. His teeth were brown and rotted, and there was an edge to him that was desperate.

"We want no trouble," I said. "Just be on yer way, an' we'll all come out o' this fine." I pulled a tiny tendril of power and pushed. *These two are dangerous. Get away from here.* The push had no effect on the man, for he let out a high cackle of a laugh.

"Hear that, Harry? The whelp is telling us to be gone." He laughed again.

The second man lifted a hand toward Aine, and I shifted sideways and put myself between them. "Get ye gone. I'll no' warn ye again." I pushed harder this time, but instead of affecting the man, I felt something inside me change.

"Get away!" shouted Aine. "Ye don't know who ye face." I heard her strained cry a moment later and realized that the first man had gone around me and now held her hard. "Let me go!" Her terror lashed my senses and the world around me wavered.

"Get yer filthy hands off her!" I shouted, turning my blade toward them. My fury grew as Aine's thoughts flit back to her uncle, and I saw images of Aine bruised and bleeding.

All at once the clearing grew hot and steam wafted up off the ground. Fear buffeted me from several directions, but the strongest came from Aine. She was now not only frightened of the man who held her, but of me as well. I was out of control. Nothing was stopping the rise of power streaming toward me and spilling through my mind. And worse, the terror she felt became my own and both grew rapidly beyond bearing.

A blinding riot of color flashed and an eerie echo of wind shrieked. The world dropped away, and I was suspended in a solid field of black as voices came at me from all sides.

"Find the boy and the talismans and bring them to me! The Templars will rue the day they chose to do battle."

"But what about the Pope? The Templars answer only to the Holy Father. We have no authority."

"We have all the authority we need. See to your end of the bargain and I will see to mine."

When I woke I first noticed the cold. Aine was bent low over me, emptying our water skin onto my face and chest. My head pulsed so badly, I was afraid that it had split in two and the contents had dumped all over the ground. I tried to sit but it was impossible.

"What are ye doin'?" My throat was raw.

"Tormod?" The light of the sky seemed to have filled her eyes. "Are ye all right?"

"I think so." I struggled to sit and only then noticed the woods around us. The earth was completely dry for a wide swath of the land and smoke curled from the edges of blackened leaves.

"What happened?" I asked fearfully.

"Ye drew the power," she said, mopping my face with the plaid. "I tried to contain it with my song, but I think I made it worse."

"Are they dead?" I held my breath, waiting for her answer.

She laughed, surprising me as nothing else could have, and brushed a tear from her eyes. "Just singed a bit. I wish that ye could have seen their faces, Tormod." She made an undignified snort and I smiled weakly. "Like rabbits. They couldn't get away fast or far enough." I was sick from using the power, but somehow her amusement eased my pain.

"Ye spoke. Near on the end of it all."

"What?" Her words seemed to echo softly in my head and none of this made sense.

"Ye said a word, or a name, perhaps. De Nogaret."

I thought on the vision. This time it had been only the disjointed sound of conversation with no images at all. "Ye're sure that was the word? I don't remember it."

She nodded. "Let's move on before they pluck up their courage and come back."

The landscape was almost too bright for my eyes. I wavered. My response to the use of the power was much, much worse this time. She had to nearly lift me, and it took us both a good long time to get back into the saddle.

When finally we set out again, I felt Aine tremble against my back. Thoughts of my loss of control haunted our every league. How could this have happened to me? I wished for the hundredth time that the Templar had not passed on and left me alone. He would have known why this was happening and what to do to remedy it. I missed him.

A DISCOVERY

Moving into the mountainous Highlands, I was colder than I could ever have imagined feeling. My fingers and toes were numb. And as the land crept ever upward, it grew worse. We rode a snaking path between the great green swaths of slope and stopped only to replenish our water and take short breaks when we needed them most. By late afternoon we'd reached the outskirts of the village of Kintore and I was nearly falling from my seat.

"I have to walk," I said. My voice was gritty and my vision seemed to pulse along with the beat of my heart.

"I could use it as well," she said. "I've never in my life ridden this long." She wobbled when her feet hit the ground. "I can barely feel my legs for the cold, an' my tailbone aches like the devil." I nodded. Though I'd ridden for long stretches before, I was out of practice. Everything hurt, even my fingers where they bent and grasped the leather of the reins. The road was uneven and narrowed sharply as we turned the bend. Aine walked ahead of the horse and me.

As we passed the first croft, what struck me most was the lack of activity within. There were no animals beside or behind the dwelling, no bairns shouted from inside, and no elders hung about the front walk. It was eerie and we both slowed as we approached.

"All is no' well here," I said. Aine had lapsed into silence. Her face was white and still.

"Can ye feel it?" she said, wrapping her arms tight around her middle.

"No, I canno'. What d'ye feel?" I asked, watching her eyes grow wide and distant.

"They came by night. Groups of soldiers. There was resistance. They killed them all."

Her hands grasped tight the folds of my plaid as she fought to see the vision that was taking hold of her. "Men. Here and again farther down the lane. *Hide. Don't speak a word. Stay here. Stay hidden.*" A chill rippled along my spine. Her voice had taken on a frightening aspect. It was as if she were someone within the vision. Her movements mimicked the speaker.

And then she was back, staring at me with wonder. And before I could question her, she bolted away, up the path and over the hill. I dropped the reins and ran as fast as my weakened legs would carry me. Her destination was the door of a hut set back from the road.

"Aine! What are ye doin'? Ye canno' go running about. It's dangerous. Stop!"

She paid me no heed. Nor did she even acknowledge that I'd spoken. I hurried to catch her before she got into trouble. My heart was near beating double time, the sweat beading upon my forehead and beneath my tunic. She was already inside when I reached the doorpost. "What the devil are ye up to, lass?" I shouted, gasping for breath.

"Shh," she said, holding her hand up to forestall my approach. Inside the hut it was dim. Though it was early afternoon, the shutters were closed up tight and the only light spilled through the door behind me.

"It's all right," she said softly.

"What's all right? Have ye gone daft?" I asked, exasperated.

She motioned quick and sharp to me. I had no idea what she was on about, but it was beginning to annoy me. I was cold and tired and in no mood for games. She had crossed the room and was bent low, speaking to a drape of linen hanging from a table in the corner.

"What —"

"Hsst," she said to me. Then, "You can come out now, dearlin'. No one here will hurt ye."

I took a step farther into the hut and shoved the door wide as Aine gently pulled the linen from the table.

Shock was the mildest of the feelings that careened through me, and confusion and worry followed fast. Enormous blue eyes peered out from the depths of the gloom. I should have felt the wean's life force long before I did, but to me, it was as if he had just flickered into existence before us.

"Come ye now, little man. We're here to help," she coaxed.

The bairn scuttled back as far as he could, pressing himself against the stone wall.

"Ye try," she said, turning to me for help. "He's sore frightened."

I approached slowly and crouched down to his level. "It's all right, laddie buck. Come to Tormod an' we'll have a bit of a play." I sent the barest tendril of power into his mind, careful to hold back, determined to keep my rogue gift in check.

The little one said nothing but moved reluctantly into the faint light, his eyes wild. I lifted my hand slowly and he scrambled away, whining soft whimpers. Aine stood frozen, barely breathing.

"I'm just goin' to see if yer hurt. It's goin' to be well, laddie. Just be still," I coaxed. He leapt away from me as if my touch burned and clung to Aine, who was nearly bowled over by his sudden advance.

"Hush, laddie. Aine's here. All is well," she said in a soothing voice.

I stood awkwardly, feeling out of place and somewhat offended that he preferred her over me. I heard her hum then, lacing the air softly.

The bairn's eyes were the blue of a clear day's sky, his hair golden threads of silk, but his face was smudged with dirt and he smelled as if he had voided where he hid. Near as I could tell he was around the mark of three, but that was the extent of the information we could gather. No matter what we said or did, no matter the question or his need, the bairn would not speak.

He did not protest when Aine took him to the well and washed him up. He did not ask for food or drink but gobbled up anything she put in his fingers. With his hand in hers, we wandered the path that ran along the nearby huts.

DESERTED

No one greeted our arrival. It was as if the whole of the place was emptied in one swift upending.

Finally, we sat on the hill beyond the last hut with the bairn curled up on Aine's lap. His thumb was tucked in his tiny mouth and his eyes were drooping.

"Well, what are we to do with him?" I asked, watching her run her fingers along the soft glint of his hair.

"We've got to take him with us, of course. He'll starve otherwise." Her head was cocked to the side at that angle I'd come to recognize as the start of a fight. This was a point she was not going to back down from. Not that I could figure any way around it.

The soft suckling of his thumb and the gentle cry of birds in the distance lulled me toward sleep. My body was sluggish and I found it difficult to think. "Let's go inside and rest," I suggested. "No one is about to protest us being here and it's safe for the moment." I stood, automatically reaching for the bairn. He squirmed away, even with his eyes closed.

"Suit yerself," I grumbled.

Aine hefted his small form into her arms, and he snuggled trustingly against her chest.

"Can ye tell anything more o' the place an' what happened?" I asked.

" 'Twas recent, mayhap yesterday even. I can feel violence. Anger. Soldiers came through and ransacked the village. Most of the men had gone off already to fight.

An' so it was the old ones and the women and bairns who stood against them. 'Twas a slaughter, Tormod. They went hut to hut, killing an' taking whatever they found." She shuddered. "I can see it as if I were standing off to the side watching and listening."

I could feel the pain and disgust the vision brought her. It was within me, filling my thoughts and muddying my mind. "Aine, yer emotions are strong. Too much for me to bear in this condition." She began to hum and I relaxed.

"Where are the bodies?" I asked when again I could speak.

"Beyond the hill." She gestured with her head and I turned. I wasn't sure why I hadn't noticed it before. A good number of birds were gathered beyond the rise, winging in circles.

"Can ye no' see an' feel what has happened here? To me 'tis as clear as daylight," said Aine.

A flicker of irritation rolled through me. "I don't have visions that come to me as yours seem to." I stared at the birds. "There are times that I see the past, but most oft I see the future. An' it's usually incomplete an' random. Ye seem to see full an' clear. Most times I hear voices and only scraps of image. I never get a whole read o' something. I'm always left to riddle out what I see and make choices from what I guess is right."

I felt lacking, admitting her gift appeared stronger than mine. It annoyed me. "Who d'ye think moved them?" I said to distract myself.

"Their men returned," she said softly.

We were quiet a moment. "Seeing just a part seems troublesome," she said. I was about to argue but she went on. "But then, what good is it to see what's gone on before? Mine is rarely of use," she said.

She started up the hillside, away from the hut we had found the bairn in, to another that stood sentinel in the twilight. I followed.

It was small, just a single room of stone with a thatched roof that had been poorly tended. I opened the door and she carried the bairn inside and laid him on a pallet in a corner.

"Can ye tell from your read o' this place where the tinderbox might be? That would be helpful," I said with an unexpected caustic edge. I smiled to ease the bite.

She returned the smile, tentatively. "No, but I think ye could go get the horse an' yer pack while I find us something to eat."

I heard the rattle of pots and trenchers as I went out and back down the hill. It was good to have a few moments' peace. Worry over my lack of control, the loss of Aine's family and the Templar, and evading our hunters was distant. I was beyond tired. It had only been days, but I felt like I'd been on the run for a sennight. I found the horse grazing in a spot of grass near where I'd left him hobbled behind the hut. By the time I got back Aine had gathered a few potatoes, onions, and some lard she found in the cupboard. I lit a small fire in the pit and Aine fried up the vegetables. The warm heaviness felt good in my stomach. Aine brought me a blanket. I couldn't seem to move from the chair by the fire. She curled up, pulling my plaid over her and the bairn on the pallet nearby. "We should put out the fire," I said.

"Later," she mumbled, drifting. "Too tired." My eyes focused on the spill of her auburn curls against the brightness of his golden locks. It was a pleasing sight that followed me when my eyes slid shut.

The quiet of the night was broken by the sound of horses along the road and I came awake fast. The slide and clink of swords and the creak of leather echoed in my ears. I crawled quickly to the pallet and slid my hand over Aine's mouth. I spoke directly into her ear as my fingers connected with her lips. "Be still, men approach."

Her body stiffened and she slid from the pallet to the floor, pulling the bairn with her. I heard her whisper words of comfort, but I couldn't tell if he understood, or even heard.

I could feel the growing excitement of our mount. There were other animals about and he was ready to join them. *Be still, lad. Be silent.* I took a calming breath and sent the lightest push I could manage. His simple mind was suddenly shuttered with peace.

I could hear the conversation outside as the men got closer.

"I smell a fire. Someone has been here," one said. I cursed our stupidity.

"We've a schedule to meet and I heard there's places along this road what's been cleared by illness," said another.

"There's no bodies here," replied the first. "An' I smell food."

My hand was tight on my dagger as the footsteps moved closer and a wash of gravel slid and bounced. They were outside, just beyond the door.

Aine's frightened gaze locked on mine and she held the bairn close, rocking. Silent. His panic was cutting me up inside, building by the moment. My head was growing hazy. *No, don't give in.*

I called the power then and grabbed a mental hold of a bit of our fear and sent the push of it right into the mind of the approaching stranger. *Illness lies here. Enter and die.*

From beyond the door I heard a gasp, then the clatter of feet as they scrambled away and down the slope. "Don't go in there. I've got a bad feeling. Sickness. Can ye not smell it? Can ye not taste it?" The man's babble was nearly hysterical.

"I smell something good. An' I'm hungry," whined another.

Quickly I sent the fear his way, not bothering to dull it as I had the first. My head was splitting up the middle. It felt as if my eyes were near to bursting and I could not hold it much longer. The room was fading.

Aine added a soft hum to my push. The second man yelped and bolted down the incline.

"Get out. Go on, quickly! This place is no good," he shrieked.

My breath rasped in the new quiet as I lay on the pallet, drifting in and out of consciousness. I could feel Aine moving about but could not lift my eyelids to see what she was doing. This time recovering was not easy. The pulse in my head beat like a bodhran. All I could do was lie still, grit my teeth, and pray the pain would go away.

I felt the bairn approach and opened my eyes. He stood before me, his gaze open and curious. Then without a word he climbed in beside me, curled up, and I felt the weight of his head on my arm. I pulled him close and thought of home as I lapsed into dreaming.

"Tormod?" Aine's soft voice dragged me back from the rest I so needed. It took much to pry my lids open.

"I think we should be gone from here. It's too close to the road. There will be others, just as there have been these. I sense in ye a weariness that should not be put to the test."

Her words made me feel as if I were lacking in something. Was it not enough that I turned away the men who had found us? I didn't say anything, just detangled my limbs from the bairn's and slowly climbed to my feet. The interior of the hut tilted, and I had to grasp the edge of the table to stay upright.

"I refilled the skins from the well and replenished our supplies." Aine tossed two apples to me in quick succession. I fumbled to catch them. The bairn was awake, watching me solemnly. I handed him one and he began to eat it with great seriousness. I wondered what he had seen and what I could do to bring him some peace. It would be foolish to try anything with the power.

Aine moved about, oblivious to my discomfort, readying for the next of our journey.

Our journey. I wondered how it had come to be that. It seemed forever my lot to stumble into situations that I had not intended. Exhausted, I sat on the pallet and let my head drop.

"Let's go," said Aine impatiently. I was not sure how long she'd been standing there. The bairn's tug on my hand finally moved me.

Beyond Aine the gray morning filled the doorway. The land was still and the cold slipped around us, seeking skin, making the small of my back quiver. "He will need more than what he has on," I said, looking down at the bairn. "Have ye woolens?" I asked.

He said nothing and merely stared at me with his enormous blue gaze. I knew he understood what I asked, but his quiet refusal to answer bothered me. "A heavy sark?" I asked again. "If ye're to come, we need to keep ye warm."

Fear flickered in the depths of his eyes, though I was not sure if it was the thought of coming or that he would be left behind. His hut was along the road we had already traveled, and I did not want to have to go back. Aine solved the issue before it became a problem.

"There are blankets here, an' a small plaid that will do. An' here's a tunic to pull over his own, an' stockings to double up." She led the bairn aside and began to bundle him.

Though I knew we could not leave him behind, the delay and my illness were making me snappish. "Could ye move it along, then?" I said irritably.

"Clapper yer gob," she snapped back. "Aren't I doin' the best I can? It wouldn't hurt ye to pack the bags back on the horse, an' see that he's watered and eaten enough of the grain I left with him. Would it?"

Her tone annoyed me quite readily. My head was pulsing with an ache behind my eyes, and I felt bleary with fatigue though I had just arisen. "We ought to just go back to one of the huts off the road and rest today," I said as I brought the horse around and fumbled to tie our packs to the buckles of the saddle. "We're better off here than any unknown place along the way."

She glared at me, her face livid. "It's no' safe here." Her words came between clenched teeth and her eyes shifted pointedly to the lad.

"For the devil's sake," I said, exasperated, "what d'ye mean to say? Out with it already."

She patted the little one's head and set him on the stoop of the door frame. "Now ye just set here for a moment, dearlin'. We're just goin' off to have a bit o' a chat." He reached for her hand, clearly frightened. "Right over here. Back before ye can count to ten." He let go reluctantly.

She grabbed my hand and tugged roughly, indicating I should follow her down the slope. I would have argued but the moment her fingers enclosed mine the worst of my aches dulled. I clutched her hand, and she shot me a look but said nothing until we were out of his hearing.

"Can't ye see that we've got to get him away from here?" she whispered furiously.

"Why?" I matched her tone.

"Because, ye dolt, I read the memories o' his hut. They killed his brothers and sisters, and his old grandy there before him. We have to take him from here. Can ye no' see that he's terrified?" Her eyes bore into mine with accusation.

I felt badly then for not seeing, not noticing how the place was truly affecting him. When I looked to the stoop I saw that he had drawn his knees close to his chest. His thumb was burrowed deep in his mouth, and his eyes were blank and staring.

I turned to her, contrite, but the superior look on her face wiped away the feeling. "Well, it's no' like I could read the scene. Ye might have shared it a bit sooner!" I didn't wait for her reply but stalked back toward the bairn.

"Hist!" I nearly felt the venom she aimed at my retreating form, but was pleased to get the last word in.

INCONSOLABLE

The bairn did not acknowledge my return. His eyes were screwed shut and his slender body rocked in time with some far-off internal rhythm. I stooped to gather him into my arms when all at once he let out a cry that rose the hair on my neck.

"What did ye do?" Aine demanded. "What's wrong?" she yelled over the wails that took over after the first scream.

Memories poured from the lad, overwhelming my senses. "He's locked in the memory," I gasped, shaking him a little. "Here now. There, there. You're all right, lad. Hush ye now."

He continued to wail and sob with no sign of stopping. Aine had covered her ears with her fingers and paced, agitated. "Can't ye do something?" she shouted.

"I don't know," I said anxiously. "I've not been trained to heal and I'm in no good state myself." The words were truer than I let on. I was a mess and the lad's trauma was combining with my own.

"I don't care. Do something! He's breaking my heart." Tears for the bairn rolled down her face. Her hurt, his fear, all too much. It had to stop.

"Here, take my hand and no matter what happens do not let go of me."

For once she had no words, no questions or chatter. She quickly latched on and immediately the peace I felt whenever she touched me returned. I took the hand of the bairn then and focused my attention on the levels of power in the soil at my feet.

The earth was rocky and the ground long trampled. The energy was deep below the surface, but I could see the network of silken strands that crossed and wove. Focusing on the peace that Aine exuded, I tugged a tendril of power. For some reason it felt strange beneath my probe. Like the dew that coated the morning grass, it beaded and scattered as I tried to call it toward me. Frustrated, I focused more sharply and felt the blood in my body race.

Somewhere off in the distance, I recognized Aine's humming. And then, as if it were the simplest thing in the world, the power came to me. Without the chaos to confuse things, the energy pulsed into my mental grasp and in turn I directed it into the mind of the bairn.

Immediately, I was immersed in his memories. Brutal images fluttered against my mind, like the frantic beat of the trapped wings of a bird. I pushed through, reaching into his past for anything that might calm and comfort him. Memories of life before, people he knew and loved, places that were special to him, and then I found it.

The doll was not much more than a pile of scraps. Leftover linen, thread for the mouth, tiny tin buttons for eyes. Its smock was worn thin from use. The image was strong. Safety and love clung to its memory like cobwebs in a corner. I seized on it and pressed it into the fore of his mind.

The lad became still quite suddenly, and I knew that I had found his comfort. I sent the image to Aine so that she would understand. Her humming paused for a moment and she gasped. Then she let go of my hand and bolted off down the road.

My mind reeled with the sudden loss of contact. Energy swirled within me, and riots of tension rolled through me. The bairn's terror came again, and this time it was more than I could bear. I was crashing, over-whelmed by the emotions piercing my mind. I needed to let go of him. I pushed away, desperate to make it stop. My ears were filled with a furious buzz and my heart pounded with pain.

Then, without warning, I saw him, my vision sharp and clear. *Alexander!* I screamed as the chaos enfolded me. *Ground, Tormod! Focus and shield the power away. Let go!*

I shoved with all my heart and mind, pushing the energy, the power back down into the ground at my feet. The land rumbled, the path split, and the bairn and I were knocked apart.

I lay stunned by the suddenness of it all. The vision of the Templar, so much as I had seen him last — strong, real, whole — hung before me. "Thank you," I whispered to whatever had brought him to me.

Aine's running footfalls pulled me from myself and suddenly anger replaced my calm. "Why did ye let go of me?" I bellowed, unable to control the wrath. "I told ye no' to let go! No matter what!"

Aine's face was a most unnatural white, and her chest heaved with the exertion of her run. I turned to see what she was staring at.

And the world roared. The bairn lay still and unmoving, his body twisted at a strange angle.

"No!" I screamed, scrambling to him. How could it be? He was so still. I laid my hands on his tiny chest and felt for his breath, but there was nothing. Tears blurred my vision and torment filled my heart. I called on the power.

Please, Lord, help! But nothing stirred. It was as if the Lord and the land had given up on me.

"No, no, no," I moaned. He could not be gone. My guilt was so deep, my pain and Aine's so hot I felt as if I might burst into flame. I couldn't think. "I killed him," I gasped, not wanting to accept that it was true.

Aine's hands were fisted on my shoulders. "No," she whispered, "I did. Ye told me no' to let go." Her words ended on a sob. "I only meant to get him his dolly. I only meant . . ." She broke down, her cries like those of a wounded animal.

I knew her thoughts. Her pain rushed through me like wildfire — the deaths of her family, the guilt she carried, her devastation over the bairn. My senses shrieked, and the power of the land suddenly broke free, welled up beneath me, and flowed through me.

With new clarity I moved deeply into the mind and body of the bairn. I saw the stillness of his tiny heart, the quiet emptiness of his mind. The power had done this. I saw the scorched places in his body where the energy had seared. I tried to fix him, as I had healed the Templar's nephew, Seamus, but I knew in my heart of hearts that he was beyond me.

It was a long while later when I realized that Aine was shaking me, and so much longer before I was able to still the tears that flooded my world.

SHAME AND GUILT

We worked in silent numbness. The day lengthened as I dug a shallow grave with an old spade from one of the huts. The ground was cold and hard. It took much to make the barest of dents, but I did it while Aine gathered stones to make a cairn.

As the rain began once more to fall, I laid his small body to rest. Aine put the doll in his hands, her tears dripping down on his pale face.

"Lord, take this innocent unto your care. He's seen more than his share an' yet not nearly enough o' this world. Though we knew him not long, he will stay with us always." I could barely speak for the sadness.

"Hail Mary, full o' grace . . ." Aine began the prayer and I joined in softly. The bairn was home with his family now.

We did not linger in that place. Aine climbed astride our horse and I walked, leading, following the road away. Sadness hung around us like the fog blanketing the mountains.

"I don't know how that could o' happened," Aine said in a whisper, as if she spoke to herself. "He was here and now he's no'." Her voice caught in a sob that she pulled back with a hiccup.

I had no answer. I couldn't speak. If I opened my mouth, I was afraid I might start screaming and never stop. I was supposed to be his protector. Instead I had killed him.

Misery and guilt were my only companions as I thought of what happened again and again, wondering what I could have done differently.

The echo of his cries filled my head. My body was cold, and my legs stumbled every few steps.

"Tormod! What's wrong? What is happening?" I felt her hands on my arms and her nails digging. Her face was strange and far away. My head pulsed with a throbbing that encompassed my eyes. I stared at her mutely, trying to make sense of what she was saying.

Focus. Ground. Shield. Words pounded my skull, but like puffs of cloud, they brushed me but beyond that had no effect. The voice in my head was not my own. I squinted. The light was too bright. I was confused. *Do it! Now!*

Aine's face was fading in the brightness of the light. *"Holy Mary, Mother of God . . ."* The words came to me, as did the vision. I saw a block of wood. Shavings curl and fall. A likeness unfolding. Dark hair and amber eyes. The face of a woman. The carving had come to life.

I blinked and my shielding was in place. Aine was before me, and the woman was gone. "I'm sorry," I whispered, and ragged sobs tore from my throat. For the bairn, for the Templar, for Seamus. For myself.

Aine took my hand and pulled me to her and hugged me. I cried a flood of tears that had no beginning or end. And for a very long time she did not let go.

As if by silent accord we spoke no more about what had happened to the bairn, and we took to the road with an emptiness I had never felt before. We walked side by side, leading the horse and holding each other's hand.

"Tormod," she said after a very long while, "I'm frightened for ye." Her nervousness slid along a path inside me and I opened my hand to pull away, but she gripped it hard. "No, don't." Her eyes beseeched mine. "Tell me what is happening. This isn't right," she said quietly.

How could I explain it? I walked along, breathing the early evening air and listening to the wind. "After ye sing, or whatever 'tis ye do, d'ye feel like yer sick or tired?" I asked.

She looked thoughtful for a moment. "Tired, surely," she said. "Ye mean it has something to do with the power?"

"Aye. The power gives us the abilities that we have, but it also takes something away each time we use it. It's like we're used as well."

She nodded, as if what I said unlocked a question she had. "An' this has something to do with the way ye are ill?"

"Aye. I think so. When I use the power, it drains me badly. I have more abilities than I ever had before. I feel the emotions of everyone around me, and I sometimes hear their thoughts." She started and made to pull her hand from mine. "No, it's all right. I canno' hear yers, an' it hasn't happened for a bit, anyway. My brother Torquil had the same response."

Aine smiled and seemed to relax in that.

"It's just that everything is so much stronger and so much more draining of late, that 'tis hard to bear." I shook my head in frustration. "Emotions seem to come at me instead o' rolling off an' away. They get tangled up with whatever I'm feeling an' they grow in me. Everything spins out o' control. I can't seem to do anything about it. Things just go awry."

Aine was quiet, her eyes fixed on the road. My thoughts drifted back to the bairn and my heart dropped even lower than it had been.

"Yet, when we touch ye seem better," she said.

"Aye. It's the only thing keeping me stable. I've only known a few of the gifted. None did that for me."

She looked down on our twined fingers. "It's a strange bit, no denying that. But as I told ye, I can usually calm folk with my hum. It must be a part o' it, though its never been like this before. I wish that I could do something more. If maybe I'd known sooner, then . . ." Her voice was strangled and she didn't continue.

Filled with sadness I said, "Aye. I wish many things, but the wishing's never done me any good. I have to warn ye. Sometimes I get pushed into a dark place that I canno' get out o'."

"Like that day on the beach, when I found ye," she said. "An' after with William?"

"Aye," I replied.

"That's frightening. Maybe using the power too

114

often has done this to ye. Maybe neither of us should use it at all," she suggested.

"It's no' that easy. I can't stop myself. The visions come when they do. Can ye stop yerself?" I asked.

"I can't stop the readin' of a place, but I can choose no' to give comfort with the song. Though when someone is in need, I wouldn't want to withhold giving them what relief I could."

We were quiet then, each lost to our own thoughts. The silence was welcoming. In it I felt no accusation, no press for what I could not give. It decided me. "I want to tell ye something, for ye have to know what danger yer in, should ye choose to stay with me."

She lifted her brow. "I'm no' goin' anywhere."

"Ye might change yer mind," I said. "I'll tell ye a story," I said, "that stretches back a good long time. It will take a bit . . ." I hesitated.

"We seem to have nothing but time," she said.

I nodded. The sound of the horse's hooves played in my ears. I felt a mess, as if I might be sick at any moment, and the light hurt my eyes.

"There was a knight. A good and brave, gifted man. His abilities were to see the future. No' just the things that would be, but also what might be."

Aine stared ahead, but her concentration was rapt.

"He came to my village on the celebration o' Beltane and asked me to deliver a message." I laughed without mirth. "And I bungled the task, as I do most things." The reminder of the bairn sent a fresh jolt of pain through me.

Aine squeezed my hand and I continued. "But in spite of it, or maybe because of my mistake, I ended up on a quest that took us far from home with bad people chasing us."

I was quiet a moment, remembering all that we'd been through and how it had turned out. It was impossible to sum up in words.

"Tell me about it," was all she said.

I nodded. We remounted the horse and I began the story from the very beginning.

A KNIGHT'S TALE

The land passed by in a blur as I spoke, and I left out no detail in the telling this time. Aine said nothing throughout the whole of it. I finished as the sun slipped from the afternoon sky.

"I know o' this thing, this carving, o' which ye speak," Aine said timidly.

"What? How?" I asked, shocked.

"When I healed ye, back a' the byre. I saw it in yer

dreams when I sang to ye." She seemed ashamed by the admission.

"Ye knew, all this time? Why didn't ye say anything?" I asked.

"I didn't know what it was or what had happened to ye, but I saw it. No' for long, but oh, it was so lovely," she said. "I didn't want ye to think I was intruding on yer memories. 'Twas no' on purpose, I swear." I could feel her agitation.

"It's all right. Sometimes that happens to me as well. I know how it can feel, like ye've listened to something ye shouldn't an' know it's wrong." I felt her relax.

"D'ye have the Holy Vessel still?" Aine asked.

"No. I gave it over to the Order at Balantrodoch." The sharp memory of the vision where soldiers rode through the gates of the preceptory and questioned the Abbot surfaced in my mind.

"And yet ye're still hunted," she said. "Why?"

"I don't know. I have to believe they didn't find what they were looking for at the preceptory. I don't even know where it lies."

"So we seek the healer ye met on yer journey," she said. "D'ye believe he can make ye well?"

"I don't know. He's fair good at what he does, but even if he canno', at least I know that he can get me to the Templars, if no' here then in France or Spain. They will protect me from the King's men.

"Aine, I shouldn't have taken ye with me. Ye could fare badly in all o' this. Finding Bertrand might be impossible, an' I am getting more an' more dangerous to be around every day. I meant it when I said ye might choose another path to travel. Mayhap ye should go yer own way." I said the words, but the thought of Aine not being with me to block the chaos filled me with panic.

"Yer no' more dangerous than the man I left," she said softly.

"I could be," I countered.

She shook her head and a dark bleakness flit through her. "I'm a fugitive now, as are ye. I think we were meant to find each other."

Her words were so similar to ones I had uttered to the Templar that I stared at her.

"What, ye don't think so?" Her voice held the edge of peevishness. It was amazing how her temper could rise with so little reason. I shrugged, disturbed by the thought that she'd compared me to her uncle. Was I a beast like him? Would I harm her? Not on purpose, surely.

"Ye need me, Tormod MacLeod," she declared.

"Aye. Perhaps." I knew that I did, but it felt distinctly unmanly to admit it.

She huffed and it gave me a small smile. It felt good to bait her. As if maybe things were not quite as dire as they might be.

A ROOM TO LET

As the last ember of daylight faded into a deep gray night, we came to the outskirts of a village. Dark crofts dotted the land and an inn sat low in a clearing. I'd become accustomed to Aine's emotions flitting in and out of my head at will, but was taken aback at the harsh flood of thoughts and feelings that assaulted me from the many who had gathered in the place.

"I canno' go farther," I gasped, grasping my head as if to contain the dizziness that almost made me retch. I drew up near the stables.

"I will go. Stay here," she said. "Do you have coin?"

"Aye." I gave her Torquil's pouch. "We need a room as far from the main road as ye can get it. Out here with the animals, mayhap." She nodded and leapt down, leaving me swaying from the sudden loss of her. "Hurry. Please."

Aine's alarmed expression met mine. "Will ye be all right?"

Her concern played havoc with my nerves. I forced myself to nod and tucked my hands beneath my arms to still the tremors so that she would not see. I slid from the horse and buried my head in his mane as she bolted along the path and disappeared into the inn.

The wait was awful. The roar of chaos from the inn was nearly deafening. Then, one feeling grew more insistent than the others. Fear spiked through my body. Aine!

I pushed it away and focused on the source, trying with my exhausted mind to read the situation and not race wildly inside. Whatever was happening was not life threatening, not trivial, but worrisome enough that her heart sped and her blood raced.

I scrambled down the path and hid near a window whose shutter was left loose to the air and peered cautiously inside. Surprise nearly felled me. Sprawled on the benches inside were the soldiers who had pulled alongside my da's boat.

Aine's back was rigid. She recognized the danger. One of the soldiers was speaking to her, and the leap of her pulse set my own to hammering. The room was loud — the scraping of chair legs and the volume of chatter kept me from hearing what he said to her. Frustrated, I stared at her back as she spoke to a heavyset woman, the mistress of the house, no doubt. Her gestures were small and neat, and she gripped Torquil's bag of coin so tight her hand was white. The mistress nodded toward the cauldron and then to the wooden trenchers by the door.

Aine moved slowly around the men. I could feel her trying to seem small and plain. I wanted desperately to add a push, a whisper screen that would flesh out the illusion, but in my current state I didn't dare.

Aine passed a thin, poxy soldier at the table's edge, and he whipped his hand out and grasped her wrist. I nearly shouted at the twist of fear that leapt from her to me. It called on the fury that seemed now forever just below the surface of my mind. With everything in me I pressed it back, feeling the splash of red hotness expanding like a team of demon horses demanding freedom.

Then, suddenly, a heavy wooden spoon landed on the back of the man's wrist and he let go. Anger sparked in the dim gray of his eyes. "Not in my establishment lest ye'd like me to remove bits o' yer parts and feed 'em to the dogs." Her voice was loud and carried to where I stood.

A giant of a man emerged from a door off to the left then and stood with arms crossed, his chest bulging a threat without words. The thin man turned away from Aine, but his eyes continued to smolder. I watched as she filled the trenchers, her back tight as a rod, ready to drop them and bolt should the need arise.

With all my might I tried to disperse the anger that hung like fine netting over me. Aine moved to the door, and as the stranger's eyes followed her, it was all I could do to force myself to step away from the window.

By the time she reached me, worry pulsed between us. I followed her to the stables without a word, opening my senses enough to seek the presence of the thin man. He remained with the others, no doubt under the watchful eye of the inn's mistress, but his intent was clear. He would come seeking Aine the moment he could do so without detection. I felt for my dagger. I would use it to protect her, that much I knew about myself now.

ANOTHER TOLL

"Sit near," Aine said, dropping to a pile of hay. I did but hesitated to touch her. She nudged her knee to my thigh and a good deal of the chaos dropped off. "We both know it helps, Tormod. No sense being squeamish about it now."

I nodded. It wasn't that I was uncomfortable touching her, but because I was on overload, her thoughts were leaking beyond my shielding. She was frightened and memories of her uncle were tormenting her. It was a trespass that I could read her and I wasn't sure if I should tell her. Even so, I needed her calm desperately. "What did ye find out?"

"There are soldiers inside," she said. "They were talking about the one they were tracking and how he had somehow slipped their grip. They were angry, but set to move on to the north to Kildrummy, I heard one say. Are they the ones? Are ye the one that got away?"

"Aye." Kildrummy lay between us and our destination. What was I to do now? I closed my eyes, thinking, waiting for her to tell me more of what happened. When moments ticked by and she didn't mention the incident with Pockface, annoyance began to churn within me.

I could feel that it bothered her, and yet she didn't confide in me. What was I to think about that? Was she afraid I'd kill him? Did she think I was so out of control she could not look to me for help?

"How can we stay here, when they're so close by?" she asked.

The whole of my body ached and my head and ears felt full of sheep's wool. "I can't go any farther." I had to sleep and recharge, but how could I do that knowing the soldiers were here and that Aine's presence would draw at least one of them?

"Give in, then. We'll sleep for half the night and leave before they rouse in the morning." Aine slid from the hay to the ground, tugging my hand and dragging me with her. I didn't know what to do for a moment. She lay with her back pressing mine. "Ye need the peace. Take it, Tormod."

Sleep pressed heavily on the back of my eyes.

In the near blackness I awoke with a rush of confusion. Something was wrong. I lay still, tightening my grip on the dagger that, even in sleep, I kept to hand.

Breath rattled in my head. The rank smell of man wafted from beyond the door frame. Gently I lifted Aine's arm, which had found its way around my chest when she turned in her sleep. I hated to break contact but there was no hope for it.

Quickly, I sprang to a crouch. As expected, it was as if every sound in and outside increased tenfold and the thoughts and dreaming minds of the inn's guests slammed into my head. I grabbed hold of the bale nearest to balance myself and fortified my shielding as best I could. It helped somewhat, but I knew it would not hold long. I scrambled to the side of the door and felt his presence before I saw the sliver of moonlight he let in.

I'd thought about how I was going to handle this before dropping off to sleep, but I had no more idea now than I did then. His breath rasped as he took a step forward and his horrible thoughts seeped into my mind.

Anger and disgust filled me, and I brought the hilt of my dagger heavily down on his head without hesitation. The sound of his body hitting the ground brought Aine awake with a cry. She took in the scene at a glance and something fragile within her seemed to snap. With a wail she launched herself across the space between us and threw her arms around me, sobbing hysterically into my plaid.

I wrapped my arms around her, murmuring whatever came to mind. "Hush. It's all right now. I've got ye. No one will hurt ye. Let it out. Let it go." Her tears flowed endlessly as she clung and sobbed. I took comfort from her closeness, but gave back what I could.

When finally I felt her body still, I tipped her head and pushed the hair from her face. In the near darkness her eyes glistened. "It's all right. Ye're safe, but we've got to go. He's knocked out, but he may wake an' we need to be far from here."

She nodded mutely and stepped away. My head swam without her touch. I could feel my protection begin to fray. Aine grabbed our pack and my hand on the way out. "You're as pale as whey."

I had thought for a moment that I would faint, but the second our hands met I was righted. It was strange and awkward moving without letting go, but things had shifted somehow. I needed her now more than ever.

Outside we mounted the horse, Aine in front this time, and urged him off down the road. Pockface was alive. He'd have a terrible headache but no more than he deserved. The thoughts I'd shared of his made me want to hit him again. That anyone should think such things about Aine filled me with an unholy furor. I wrapped my arms tighter around her middle than I probably needed. She didn't remark on it.

The sun was climbing slowly. Pearl pink stole through the tops of ebony branches, and the smell of wetness was everywhere. I closed my eyes every few moments, leaving Aine to guide the horse. The landscape before me was playing tricks on my eyes. I saw it as it was, but also as it must have been in other times, other seasons. My mind was drifting when sound burst loud in my ears.

"*What have you to say?*"

"*The goal is within our grasp.*"

"*You have contact within?*"

"*Yes.*"

"*And he's willing?*"

"*Gold offers much in the way of persuasion.*"

Darkness flecked with golden light. The scent of hot beeswax. Tapestries woven with gilded thread. Impatience and arrogance swirled at the edges of thought. I felt myself start to slip.

"Tormod!"

Aine's voice cut through the black, and I felt her twist in the saddle and wrap her arm around me. I shook my head and light crept back before my eyes.

"What is it?" Aine asked in alarm.

"I don't know." My breath came in short bursts as if I had just run a long way, and my legs were trembling where they gripped the horse. "A vision but it was no' clear. It's never clear," I said, frustrated. "Something is happening in the world beyond. It seems to have nothing to do with me, but it must." My head was swimming and I gripped her tight.

"Are ye all right to travel? Or do we need to stop?" she asked.

I was far beyond tired, but we had to outride the soldiers. Our destination was the same, and there was not much time or distance between us. "I can make it," I said, trying to convince myself as much as Aine.

We had traded Black for a strong warhorse that had been stabled alongside him. No doubt it belonged to one of the soldiers. I hoped that it was Pockface's and that he would be inconvenienced by more than an aching head.

I said a prayer, asking God to forgive our theft. Some Templar's apprentice I was turning out to be. Stealing. Add that to the list of sins on my soul.

We rode long that day, moving as if in a dream, or mayhap a nightmare. I felt a fright. Aine convinced me to take some time and doze, but each time I tried, eyes followed me into the dream state. I saw the bairn again and again. His pain and confusion were my own, growing and building by the league. I lost awareness of the woods, of time, and of myself.

"Tormod!" Aine's stricken voice cut my stupor.

TRESPASS AT RISK

"Bit late to be wandering the roads." A tall, thickset man on horseback barred our way. I hadn't heard or seen him until Aine's cry. At his side hung a large broadsword, and two rows of throwing knives were tucked in bands across his chest. His hair was a mass of wild black tangles, and his beard flowed long down his neck and back.

I watched as he and two others who had appeared out of the woods dismounted.

"Down," he said to us.

My arms were wrapped tight around Aine. "Just do as he says," I told her, barely able to speak.

She slid from the horse and the moment the contact between us broke, my body rebelled. I closed my eyes, trying desperately to shield, but one of the men by me thought this a stalling tactic and pulled me hard from the saddle.

Inside me a red haze was building. I could feel the power rising and panic enfolding me. This man was thin, but taller than me. He easily pinned my arms and slid his dagger to my neck.

Though I could not see her, I felt Aine's terror pummeling my entire being. "What d'ye want? We have nothing." I tried to whisper a push of suggestion, but the power was flaring out of reach and control.

"Who are ye and what is yer destination?" growled the first.

To answer was almost more than I could manage. My mouth was parched and my eyes had gone dim. In my ears was a roar drowning out all sound and thought. I kept reaching for Aine with my thoughts, but she was across the clearing and I could find no relief. The man was speaking, but only a rumbling murmur reached my ears. Destination did he say?

"My sister an' I are on route to our uncle in Kindrochit," I rasped. Sweat beaded along my neck and my shivers were growing in intensity.

"Ye're lyin'," he said flatly.

He knew. How? My brain did not seem to be working right. Aine's terror pounded my head, confusing me.

"Bind an' blind them," I heard him say, and a hot surge of panic raced through me. I could not be bound. The power was rising and soon I wouldn't be able to control it. Panicked, I reached for the thoughts of the man who had spoken, but I could get nothing. It was as if a shutter had closed on my mind's eye. What was happening? I still felt Aine nearby. Her emotions were meshing with my own and driving me mad.

Suddenly a rough cloth came down over my eyes. I bucked, trying to push it away when I felt a sharp bite of pain at my neck. In a panic I began to thrash.

"Tormod, be still!" Aine cried. "Don't fight it. He has a knife."

Her voice was silenced then as completely as my sight, and hysteria filled me. I reached for the power, commanding it to come, and yet it would not. "Aine!" I shouted, straining toward her.

A new voice added to the mix, addressing me. "Hold ye now. If ye know what's good for ye, ye'll steady up. No harm is intended."

At the newcomer's words the man holding the knife to my throat stepped away. Still blind, I teetered, stumbling back over the uneven ground. Hands reached out to steady me and I automatically reached to read him. Even by touch I felt nothing. When I was able to stand on my own, he let go. Panic ripped through me then with such a vengeance I dropped to my knees and began to retch.

It was ridiculous and embarrassing to lose my stomach with all the world watching, but there was no help for it. I heaved and gagged as if my insides would turn out.

"Release her," said the leader. "Go to him."

I anticipated Aine's approach with nearly a hunger, needing her touch, but miserable that I was making a spectacle of myself.

"Give them some time. Ready the horses."

I felt Aine's hand at my back and grew faint with relief. The worst of the nausea and fear settled instantly.

"Bind them, hand to hand," the leader said.

Aine helped me to my feet and, though it might have looked odd, I gripped her hand desperately. We waited, tense and frightened. They bound her eyes as well. I knew, for she had to let go a moment as they turned and tied her. The bile began to rise again, but was forgotten almost instantly when they bound our wrists to each other. We waited in the darkness for some indication as to what was expected of us. I was weak and shaky, and my mouth tasted of dung.

Who were these men? What were we to them? I listened carefully, but the only sounds I heard were the soft rustle of footsteps, the whisper of the trees, and the soft, even shush of Aine's breath.

"You will mount up now," said the leader.

Aine and I were helped into the saddle. Around us the creak of leather and the shift of hooves signaled the crew's readiness to travel.

"Tormod," Aine whispered in my ear.

"Are ye all right?" I asked, barely able to move my lips.

"Aye."

"Yer voice cut off so quickly I thought they gagged ye," I said.

"They did, but the strange one took it off me when I mounted," she whispered in return.

"Ye felt it, too?" Our horse started forward, following the lead of the rest. "Tell me."

"I can sense nothing in him," she said. "I don't usually notice because it's just a part of the way people appear to me, but . . ."

"Aye," I said. "It's downright eerie. No emotion. No feel of life," I murmured.

"I feel the others," she said.

"They're all blank to me. The power is no' mine to command right now," I said, frustrated and frightened. "Be wary around the last. If he feels different to ye, trust that he is."

"Aye."

We rode blind, and my thoughts raced. I had never been totally without contact to the power. It was a helpless feeling. Thinking that at any moment we might be led off a cliff had my insides heaving. But there were advantages as well. Without my eyes to distract me, I heard things I might not have otherwise.

The men spoke in soft tones, yet their words came to me clearly. Aine and I had stumbled across the site of a secret meeting. They thought us spies, sent from the camp of an enemy.

The journey was long, much of it up slopes and through forest. And through it all, I felt no life from anything around me. I rode in a daze with Aine slumped against me. Exhausted, she had fallen asleep. I held her close so that she would not topple off. Time passed slowly. I had no idea what they meant to do with us. But it mattered not, there was nothing I could do about it.

Higher in the mountains the air grew colder. When I felt Aine's shiver against my chest, I wriggled my plaid free and draped it around the both of us. She slept on, oblivious, and I spent the time trying to solid up my shielding.

Near midday, we rode into a flat patch and the horses stopped. I'd been drifting in and out and came awake as Aine did.

"What's happening?" she asked, her anxiety building and taking mine with it. Men were dismounting around us, their conversations muffled.

"I don't know, but we've arrived wherever we are meant to." The snap of twigs announced the approach of someone and I pressed my legs to hers in warning.

"Ye won't be needing these," he said. The voice was the blank one. I squinted to see what he looked like as the covering over my eyes came free. He was a tall, ruddy-skinned man with dark hair and eyes. As he stared at us I had the feeling he was taking my measure. "To those who don't know them, the mountain paths are treacherous. So I'd forget the notion to run ere it comes to ye." I stared at him, trying to see what it was that made him so different, so silent. I found nothing.

It was fully dark and we were at the center of a gathering. Tents were pitched at various spots. A large fire glowed brilliantly nearby. Across its span a great spit stretched and a brace of hare was roasting. My stomach rumbled.

We were untied and helped from the horse. Aine sidled close to my side and took my hand in hers. I was glad of it, for the fear had returned as did my awareness of more men around us. Out of the loop of my plaid Aine began once again to shiver.

"Can I have our pack?" I asked the man. "We're cold."

"Haul up next to the fire," the blank one said. "We need to go through it first."

He disappeared into one of the larger tents, leaving us behind on our own. Our guards had scattered as well. No one seemed concerned that we would try to run. As I looked around I understood. We were in the middle of nowhere.

"Where are we?" asked Aine.

I shrugged and tugged her toward the fire. Her hand in mine seemed more natural now, though I wasn't quite sure when that had happened. Perhaps while riding and traveling as close as we had been. It was a good thing, for I badly needed her calming.

Several men moved about, one turned the spit and adjusted the fire, another sharpened his blade with a stone by the trees. Yet another stood, watchful, and peered back along the path we'd traveled.

"What do you make of this place?" Aine asked.

"I don't know. I can't imagine why they would have brought us along and no' killed us outright," I whispered.

We sat by the fire's edge, waiting while life continued in the clearing as if we were of no account. But for the man who tended the fire, no one noticed or seemed to care that we existed.

A long while passed. "D'ye think they're the watch?" Aine finally asked.

"I don't think so. And even if they are, what are the chances of them knowing we are wanted? It hasn't been long enough for word to reach them." I wanted to reassure her, but in truth these could be those very men. Our fate was no longer in our hands.

The flap on one of the large tents stirred and a man I had not seen before stepped into the firelight. My eyes seized on him in an instant, and my heart for no good reason skipped a beat. He approached alone, and Aine, who had been quietly complaining that she was starving, went unaccountably still.

THE OUTLAW KING

"Two alone, traveling the rough o' the Highlands. An interesting tale no doubt." His voice was smooth, even toned, and learned.

"Who are ye?" Aine asked before I had the nerve to.

"I am the Bruce," he said plainly, "Robert to those who I name friend." He tilted his head and held out his hand to me. "Can I count ye as a friend?" he asked.

"Aye, sire. It would be an honor," I said, dropping to my knees, nearly overcome with reverence. Robert Bruce, the King of Scotland, crowned at Scone on the Stone of Destiny.

He was of medium height with a long, full beard and thick, bushy eyebrows. And yet it was his eyes that distinguished him from others. They had an intensity that caught you up and snared you like a fox.

"An' would ye be a friend as well?" He addressed his question to Aine, who was deep in a curtsy. He took her hand and lifted her to stand. I felt her faintness ripple through me.

"Aye, my Lord." She smiled at him; a wide-lipped, full-toothed thing that made her eyes glow.

For no reason I could fathom, the smile irritated the life out of me. I nudged her and, leaning toward the fire out of earshot of the others, said, "Close yer mouth. Flies are drawing."

Her slight squeal preceded the elbow that jabbed my side. My yelp was not nearly as quiet and the Bruce's laugh cut the night.

"Come ye both, my new friends. Ye must be hungry," he said, leading us toward the main tent. "Geoffrey, bring some refreshments, if ye would."

The man turning the spit nodded and began to cut slices of hare onto a trencher. "Yes, my Lord."

"There's a story in this that may be as interesting as my own," the Bruce said. He lifted the tent flap and motioned us inside. "Why don't we start with yer names an' how ye've come to be with me. We'll see where it leads from there."

The tent was larger on the inside than it appeared without. Long draping swaths of canvas enclosed one enormous room that was divided into a general meeting area, cut into several spaces and curtained off at the back where I assumed his private quarters lay. Three trunks were set next to one another and wooden tables and chairs were arranged. On one, a variety of maps was laid out, tacked in place by stone chessmen.

"I am Tormod MacLeod of Leith," I said. I looked over to Aine, but she refused to turn my way. She had broken contact over my taunt and was now on the opposite side of the map table, far from me. My body was trembling without her.

"And I am Aine Cleary." Still no acknowledgment of me, or my trouble, though I was sure she knew of it. I cursed myself for a fool and wished heartily that I had curbed my tongue. The chaos was reeling through me and building, but I refused to go to her when she so obviously had decided to punish me. My annoyance at her, however, was not a good companion. It filled my mind and combined with hers, and all of a sudden the emotions of the men of the camp came to me as well. I was confused and overwhelmed.

I noticed then that everyone in the tent was staring and thought perhaps that the Bruce had asked a question, but for the life of me I didn't know what it was. The air was becoming strangely hot and the light in the tent overly bright. Blood was thrumming hard in my veins.

"Tormod!" Aine's gasped cry barely stirred the air by my ears. Before I could credit what was happening, I felt the floor of the tent rise up to meet me.

THE HIDDEN TRUTH

A buzz filled my ears like the hum of a million wings and the dim inside of a kirk filled my mind's eye. A rough altar stood at the fore and a wooden cross was suspended above. Several men moved in stealth.

"Well, I have come. What have ye to say?"

"We both know that there can only be one King of Scotland."

"And that Kingship should by rights fall to me."

"And I believe that it is mine to inherit. It matters no', I have a proposition."

"Aye?"

"That we become partners. Ye an' yer clan will become richer than ere ye dreamt possible. Lands and titles I will grant, an' ye will become my right hand. Together we will take Scotland from this English dog."

"An' I say the Comyns will rule, an' ye can be my right hand. It is as it always has been. Why the meeting?"

A whisper of movement. A rustle of cloth.

"No! This is no' the way!" The shout rang out.

Blades clashed. Men fought. A scream split the night.

"Step back, Robert!"

"Gaylen! What have ye done?"

Light rose before my eyes, bringing me fully back to the Bruce's tent and those staring down at me.

"He's coming around." A man crouched before me, but I could not feel his emotion or intent. I remembered his voice, though. *Step back, Robert!* The smell of camphor wafted into my nostrils and I swatted it aside.

"Tormod, can ye hear me?"

This voice I knew as well, from the vision and as well as from here, now: King Robert the Bruce. My mind was having trouble sorting out what I'd heard and seen. The face of the blank one was before me. He was holding my head, speaking. I saw his mouth move and remembered.

"Ye killed the Red Comyn." I couldn't believe the words had escaped me.

He flinched and stumbled back, shock and anger filling his eyes. "What did ye say?" The cold voice cut me and I was suddenly deadly afraid. Sweat built quickly and rolled down my neck.

"Nothing." Lord help me, how could I have spoken? A meeting held in secret in a kirk. This man had stabbed the rival to the throne.

Aine was at my side. I felt the twist of her fear and it built with my own, making it worse, and then suddenly I was back in the state she had found me in. My body felt dead and yet my mind was alert. This man was danger incarnate and I knew that he had killed without remorse on the altar of God.

In a panic I called for the power but it scattered from my touch. *Aine.* I sent the whisper of her name, desperate to somehow make her understand that I was here, that I needed her, but I couldn't do much more than send a word or a thought.

Her startled gasp sounded in my head and I put all I had into the reach. *Sing for me.*

In an instant her music swirled and wove around my body, loosening the bonds and bringing me back.

Focus. The command came to me as if from a dream, a memory.

I was confused. Aine's hum was softening my thoughts, but the word came again, demanding I stay on track. *Focus.*

I did and the cool wash of a breeze flit through my mind. Suddenly I found I could move my lips again.

Ground, I said to myself, and this time the power came to me, clinging to the surfaces of my inner mind, taking hold, healing.

"He's coming around!" I heard the Bruce say, and the dangerous one stepped away from me.

"Tormod, can ye hear me?"

Shield. The command seemed much closer this time, and I pushed the power outward. The shielding was not the strongest, but it was the most difficult I'd ever attempted.

Aine and the Bruce were crouched before me, but it was the cold, calculating gaze of the other that held mine. I turned away, trying to rise, but the tent tilted and a hand pushed me flat. My fear grew ever higher, but Aine took hold of my shoulders and slowly the world began to right. The ground was hard beneath me, and my body and head ached.

"How d'ye feel, lad?" It was the Bruce asking.

"Better," I gasped, not at all sure it was the truth.

"Gaylen, have we any valerian?" asked the Bruce.

"Aye. I'll have it brought to their tent." Gaylen, the blank one, the killer, helped me to sit. "Yer in quite a state," he said. His eyes were cold, unfathomable. "Why d'ye travel this road?"

"We seek a healer. I am hunted," I answered as if compelled. A strange itch filled my head behind my eyes.

"An' how is it ye knew where ye'd find the Bruce?" he asked.

"We did no'. Ye found us. We seek Bertrand Beaton, a Templar healer." I could not help but to answer his questions. The answers felt as if they were torn from my head. Aine helped me to my feet, and I immediately had the urge to flee. My eyes strayed nervously to the tent flap.

"We know Bertrand well," said the Bruce. "But ye've missed him. He's gone to Elgin."

My heart sank. "Is Elgin far?" We had to get out of here. My fears began to rise again and, as if on demand, Aine's lifted and combined and we began the spiral upward.

It was Gaylen who answered. "A lifetime away." The words were meant for me alone.

I dropped my head in despair. "If ye could tell us how to get there, we'll bother ye no more," I said. A faint was again spreading over me. My legs wavered.

"Ye're in no shape to travel. Ye'll stay with us," said Gaylen. He was not giving us the option to leave. He turned to the King then. "I would speak to ye a moment in private, sire."

The Bruce nodded and called to a guard standing outside the tent. "Is all as it should be?"

"Aye, sire."

"Yer tent is ready. Ye may both retire." The King dismissed us and a pang of uncertainty rippled through me. The ache in my head grew worse. A man came at the call of the King and escorted us outside.

"Tormod!" Aine whispered. I cut her off with a quick look and shake of my head.

We were led to a small, dark tent. Our meager pack was set beside two blankets spaced a hand span apart. It might have seemed confining if my head had hurt a little less. As it was, I was happy to fall onto the blanket and urge Aine down beside me.

He left us with a trencher of hare and some greens. The food sat untouched as I tried in vain to settle myself. Her worry was strong in my head.

"We've got to get out o' here as soon as we can. I had a vision about the Bruce and Gaylen, and I saw something I should no' have." The pull of sleep and the darkened tent beckoned.

Aine shook me. "Tell me," she said.

"I saw Gaylen kill the Red Comyn on an altar in some darkened kirk. Robert the Bruce was there. It was a meeting of some sort to try and win Comyn's support o' the Bruce as King. The discussion turned to argument an' Gaylen killed the clan leader."

"I saw it as well!" she said faintly. "We shared this vision."

Her words surprised me. How was that possible? "This vision was different. 'Twas of the past, which rarely comes to me. 'Twas clear and complete. It is never that way for me."

"It is as you describe for me, usually, except I hear no sound. This time, I saw only movement in a vague half-light and I heard everything. What does any of this mean?" she asked.

"The visions are changing. It is a part o' what is happening to me I would grant. But more than that, what we saw is no' something Gaylen would have us know."

"Aye. I've heard William speak o' the Red Comyn. His claim to the throne was strong, an' he had many supporters throughout the land," she said.

"He was ambushed," I said.

"Are ye sure? That's a dangerous thing to be speaking aloud," she said.

I hesitated. "I don't know. It happened quickly. Gaylen did the deed. The Bruce protested, but he was too late." A cold sinking feeling was strong in the pit of my stomach. "I don't think any on the Comyn side lived. There were no witnesses."

Her eyes met mine and fear trembled back and forth between us. "None, but us," she said with a shudder. "How can Gaylen know that you saw, though?"

"I spoke the words aloud when I came out o' the vision state. He heard me, I know it."

"D'ye think that's what they needed to talk about?" she asked.

"Aye. We're no' going to be allowed to leave." My head was near to splitting in pieces. Recovering was far worse than even losing control of the power. That it had happened again was beyond frightening. Something very bad was happening to me.

"I need to sleep," I said, not wanting to frighten Aine with my dark thoughts.

"Eat first," she said, shoving a piece of meat into my mouth before I could protest. It was all I could do to finish before seeking the rest that I so desperately needed.

I felt Aine at my side and without asking pulled her close and wrapped around her. Peace stole gently over me.

A WAY OUT

"Tormod!" Fear flooded my sleep-fogged brain. Aine's hand was on my arm, dragging me up.

The sound of men moving at quick pace was loud

beyond our walls. The clink of stakes and the shout of orders filled the morning air. A soldier struck the canvas side of our tent roughly. "Out! Now!" he demanded. We were being evicted.

"What's happening?" I asked, hurrying Aine out of the tent before me.

"We're moving. Our camp is breeched." His words were clipped and impatient. Aine and I were ignored as a flurry of activity flowed around us. Tents were dropped and rolled faster than I could credit. The fire was tamped and packhorses loaded. I looked for the King, but neither he nor Gaylen were anywhere about. "Let's grab a horse an' get out of here," I whispered.

"But they'll see us," she said.

Her fear was escalating inside me again. I tamped it down as best I could, but my head was pounding in moments. Aine moved close and took my hand, no doubt seeing me waver. "We won't have this chance again." Just as I spoke, the Bruce strode into the clearing, his lead men flanking him.

"Tormod, Aine. Mount up an' join the line."

I shot Aine a quick glance, knowing our time to escape had come and gone. I let go only long enough to climb into the saddle, but even that short a time was enough to nearly undo me. The activity of the many men in the camp was overwhelming. Even Aine's touch did not insulate me, and I nearly tumbled to the ground. Aine wrenched me back into position.

Gaylen appeared at our side. "Ride. Stay with the front of the line." He rode off, calling orders to others.

We moved ahead of the line just as the feel of men on the attack hit me. At least twenty strong, they pounded into the clearing with swords outstretched. The burst of their fury slammed my barely protected mind like a smith's hammer. Nearly blind, I dug my heels into the horse's sides and took off like a shot. Behind us, horses screamed. Men shouted and the clash of steel filled the air.

We raced like the devil was on our tail, skirting the horses that had turned to engage in the battle. Aine held tight, and I felt more than heard the hum that filled my ears. I didn't try to add to her pull of the power. All I could do was give the horse his head and hang on for life.

The road twisted upward and branched at several intervals. We had no idea where we were going or in what direction we should turn. Distance was our only priority. It was several leagues before I let the horse slow and the tightness in my chest and back loosen. Aine's hum had long since faded, but her fierce grip on me had not. I could feel the rapid beat of her heart as strongly as the life force of the trees around us.

We rode that way for a long time before either of us

spoke. I could tell Aine was getting ready to say some-thing. "Where d'ye suppose we are?" she asked.

Though I didn't want to admit it, I said, "I have no idea. Let's try for the top of that slope and see if anything helps," I said.

It was a long way off and I wasn't at all optimistic about the result. "It all looks the same," Aine said. "Gaylen warned that the paths in these hills lead in circles."

It did feel that way, but I didn't want to add to her worry. The day was moving on. The pale shadow of the sun that had greeted our waking was now high above, and my stomach was beginning to complain. I reached down and dug some carrots from the pack and handed her one.

"We're better off on our own than with Gaylen," I said. "I don't know what he had planned, but I'm fair sure letting us go off and find Bertrand was no' a part o' it. We'll make our way," I said, putting as much reassurance as I could into my words.

"But up here, with no direction and only a bit o' food left . . ." she said.

"We'll be fine. There's got to be game around and nuts and berries." I hadn't seen any evidence to support the thought but I needed Aine calm. Her fears were mine and when they grew, the out-of-control feeling in me did as well.

"D'ye think they won the day?" she asked. Her teeth were chattering, though from nervousness or cold, I couldn't tell. I climbed off the horse. "What are ye doin'?" she asked.

"I have some things in my pack. Ye can cover up a bit. Ye're shaking like a leaf in the wind." I fished out my extra sark. "Here. Put this on."

She slid down and shrugged into the extra layer. "D'ye think that we'll be long out here?" Her voice was small, and I found myself bothered that I didn't have the answer she needed.

"We'll make do." I didn't say that my problems using the power worried me more, or that it was possible I could go back into that barely conscious state and leave her completely alone.

The horse's sides were heaving from our flight. I ran my hands along his neck. "He's tired an' hungry. Ye go on an' remount an' I'll walk alongside." I gave the horse leave to chew at a patch of late grass. "We have no other choice but to move ahead from hill to hill. We'll follow the path o' the sun and hope for the best."

The prospect was daunting. On foot, the next summit was a long way off. "I'll walk as well," she said. "We can't afford to lame him."

I nodded. She was right. We would have to make choices from now on. The mountain pass was a thin track, stretching high into the hanging mist of the day.

The top was completely hidden by haze. "We may no' be able to see much even when we get there," she said as I took the reins and began to lead.

The air was damp and frigid. It crept into our clothing and made it impossible to stay warm. As we walked, the land swam in and out of my sight. It was all I could do to keep moving and upright.

The Bruce's men would be seeking us. The information we had was dangerous in the hands of his enemies. He had barely begun to unite the country. If word of an ambush by his people were to reach the Comyns there would be war between the clans. And it would all be to the benefit of the English King trying to conquer Scotland.

Why had the vision shown me what it had? Was it a part of the rest I had seen? There were no revelations, however, to be found among the damp trees. And yet there was a strange calm that came of walking here.

The last of the summer leaves glistened beneath the scant rays of sunlight, dark then bright. Power swirled around my ankles. There. That was the difference. I could feel the power again. It came to me more strongly with each step.

"Can ye feel any trace o' the group that attacked the camp or o' the Bruce and his men?" Aine asked.

I was startled by her voice. My mind had been drifting. "No, I canno' sense anyone, but I wouldn't count on me for that. My senses are so out o' sorts, they might be standing next to us and I'd no' feel them." Her eyes met mine. Her face was pale. "It's all right. We've put much distance between us."

Aine cocked her head, as if listening to something far away. "Does this place seem at all unusual to ye?" she asked.

The strong beat of the land was intoxicating. The power was washing through me unchecked. It was pure but a bit harsh. I couldn't seem to filter it through me right. It called to my body, and I could do nothing but go to it. I led Aine and the horse off the path and started up over the hillside in a weaving westerly movement.

"Are ye sure this is wise?" Aine asked. "Should we not stay at least on the track?" I could feel the roil of her anxiety but this time it found no purchase in me.

"Canno'. 'Tis no' on the track," I said, my words an effort.

"What's no', Tormod?"

"It's here. Up there somewhere," I said, distracted.

Aine was nervous beside me. I could feel it, but spared no energy to think on it.

We took the most direct route we could, following the pull of the power. The land was difficult — it sloped at times nearly vertical. "Listen," I said. "Can ye hear water?"

Aine was breathing hard. "No, nothing."

"Well, I do. It's coming from there." I pointed off to the left. There was a tangle of tall bushes and spindly trees blocking what lay ahead. Slowly we made our way toward the sound. Skirting the trees, I saw the stream. It was not a waterfall like the one that fronted the cave in France, but two distinct flows trickling down the hillside. They merged nearly at our feet to make a single strong current. I wondered if water had something to do with key places of power.

Like a boulder tossed in the stream . . . The phrase the Templar used to describe the way events affected the future came to me as if from far away.

A flash of light burst behind my eyes and the glint of a blade darted and swept.

I stumbled and fell against the horse's side. "What was that?" I gasped, blinking. A strange dizziness hung over me and my heart was beating fast.

"Tormod." Aine was snapping her fingers close to my eye, and truly I was not sure how long I had been standing there adrift. "Ye're frightening me."

I shook my head, trying to clear it, and started across the stream. The hillside stretched sharply upward. Looking toward the crest made my head swim.

"Where are we going? What are ye lookin' for?" Aine asked, out of breath and clearly skeptical.

"It's there," I said, nearly babbling. "Can't ye feel it?"

"Tormod. Ye're out o' sorts. Slow down." Aine's hum began softly, and when I didn't react she sang, louder and stronger. I breathed deeply. As the wind blew, the trickle of sap deep within the trees and the life of animals hidden from the rest of the world came to me in a rush. And with it came an awareness that bolted through Aine and reverberated through me. Her eyes were wide with wonder.

"Tormod, what is that?"

ANCIENT REMAINS

Atop a wide swath of green sat an ancient hill fort. It had the look of a great stone beehive whose top and front had been scooped away. An interesting thought for, coming across the slope, I felt as if a swarm of bees was circling my head. "Can ye feel the power?" I asked Aine.

She nodded, aghast. I felt as she did. The beat of the land nearly took my breath away. It was in the wind that blew strong and cutting on the flat so high above everything. It was beneath my cold and tired feet. My body was tight and ached anew with every step in its direction.

As if in a daze, we circled around to the front.

Double walls of interlaced blocks of stone two hand spans wide and one layer deep were stacked in an upward spiral. The entrance was a hole in the foremost wall that nearly reached my chest. I had to hang on the neck of the horse to bring him low enough to enter, but he didn't seem to mind, as once inside the circular courtyard the wind dropped and I left him free to wander.

He took up a spot by the exposed inner wall and Aine and I took a look about. A great tree had taken seed at sometime during the centuries of exposure. Twigs and broken limbs were scattered on the ground.

"We'd better make a torch or two. It's dark inside the walls," I said, wrapping a limb and lighting it with a spark from my flint.

"Are we going to sleep in there?"

I shared the trepidation she felt. I'd never come across a place with as much power as I could sense here. I nodded. There was a small doorway in the inner wall that came immediately to two sets of steps, one leading up and one leading down. The air inside was raw. "Which way?" I asked softly.

I didn't need to see Aine's response, I could sense it. She was frightened. "I'd rather go up. I don't know what happened down below, but I'm no' about to sleep there." In the tight space her arm pressed against mine. I was not ready for the rush of fear that leapt from her to me. It made me sweat and tremble.

I took the stairs slowly, testing my weight before moving from one to the next. They were solid, perhaps as strong as when they were originally built. The light of the torch struck the dappled walls, and their spots and shadows looked eerily like eyes watching our every movement.

We stopped at the first landing and stared out across the space. A platform had no doubt once existed here, but it had long since rotted away. We moved on and up as the stairs twisted and turned until we came to the second landing. This appeared intact and stretched to the wall opposite, but creaked ominously when I set my weight on it. "I don't trust these old timbers. We can either sleep at the ground level or go below."

A shaft of Aine's fear pelted mine. "I don't want to sleep in here at all. It's too much. I can't think straight. It sounds like bees buzzing in my head. Like the walls are screaming."

The power ebbed and flowed through the soles of my feet. I felt adrift and yet strangely desirous of finding out what lay below. "We'll sleep just inside the door." My voice sounded odd, disjointed in my ears, as if it belonged to someone else. "I'm going below to see what is there."

"Then go alone because I will not," Aine said angrily.

I left her at the door without another word, making my way as if in a dream.

The steps were small and twisted tightly. The dark was deep and dense, as if the very air was black. The light of the torch flickered as I moved, casting a dancing shadow on the mottled walls. Lower and slower with every step, I descended, the pulse of the land beating like a gigantic heart.

"Tormod?" Aine's voice was like a whisper in my head. Only the power was important now. Calling me. Drawing me.

At the last stair I became disoriented. I stumbled forward and the torch flew from my grip, sputtering out of sight. Alone in the dark I could hear my heart hammering and feel the cold seeping into my bones, making me one with the black, pulling me forward. My feet began to tingle first, and then it ran up my legs and torso. As if hundreds of midges were streaming through my blood, the power of the ancient space suffused me.

"*Where is it, boy? Tell me now and the pain will end.*" Welts of scalding heat screamed along my skin. Mewling, panting, desperate sounds rent the air.

"Tormod!" Aine shouted from above. "What has happened?"

I couldn't speak, couldn't move. And yet I heard voices and saw places and scenes within the blink of an eye. The black was like an endless doorway reaching forward and back. It was fluid, like a pond, with ripples that spread and flowed outward. Something was wrong with the energy here, and the power was demanding that I make it right. *I am not a healer,* I thought. *I am not even an apprentice.*

Then, as if in response, the power shifted. Instead of making me whole, as I knew it was trying, it reversed and I felt myself quickly unraveling. The heat diminished and a cold as I had never felt before swept through me.

A floodgate of terror expanded around me. I saw images of blood and sacrifice. The power was surging and building, but it was not for the good. "No!" I screamed. "No!"

"Tormod!"

And the dark took me away.

DRAWN FROM BEYOND

The earth was hard beneath me and soft arms enfolded my chest. A small fire burned nearby, and I saw that Aine looked perhaps as I felt.

"Where am I? What has happened?" I had the memory of her voice and a song I didn't recognize, my arms around her neck, and the persistent demand that I help her help me up the steps. My body felt as frail as a bird, and I drifted as if I were floating.

"Are ye truly alive?" her gasp was ragged, as if she'd been shouting for a very long time, and she untangled herself to look me over.

"I feel of another world." Speaking stole what little energy I had left. "I dropped the torch," I said, searching for memory in my thick and foggy head.

Aine looked at me strangely. "Aye. Ye did, but it's been days, Tormod. I thought ye'd never awaken."

I shook my head. Days. I had no notion of time passing. I started to sit, but my body would not oblige. "I can hardly move."

"Ye're weak. There was not much food and no way to get ye to swallow what I had save water. Here. Ye'll need more." She handed me the skin and it felt to weigh ten stone.

I looked around. We were just inside the doorway of the broch. "Days," I mumbled to myself. "What is this place?" I asked.

"A chamber o' sacrifice," Aine said with a shudder. "I've read much over the last few days. There is a wrongness here. Something to do with the power. Something grounded in blood."

Her words sparked a memory that came to me haltingly. "There is a place below that is damaged. A doorway of sorts, sealed by the power. It is like a lake that's been turned on its side and a stone has been dropped into the center. There are ripples and in the middle, a place that is thin," I said.

Aine lay down on her side and stared at me as if she might never blink.

"It wanted healing and tried to pull it from me, but I don't have what it needs," I said.

"Do ye know what it needs?" she asked. I shook my head no.

"I feel as if I've had a lifetime of dreams," I said.

"Ye've been like the dead, but I know o' the dreams. I sang to ye as much as I could, an' when I did yer visions became mine. Some were very unpleasant," she said. "The ones o' fire and burning were the worst." She released a long breath and her eyes wavered. "I am sore tired, Tormod. Mayhap ye could let me sleep awhile. We will speak more later." Her request had barely ended and I'd not answered before I heard the soft rattle of her breath.

I was not long behind.

When I stirred from the depths of sleep a long while later, I felt better. It was, no doubt, from having slept with Aine wrapped around me, but she was nowhere in sight. My head felt light when I crawled to my knees and then gained my feet. Bile washed the back of my throat.

"Tormod?" Aine called from outside.

"Aye." It was agony to answer. I heard her steps come near and in moments she was beneath my shoulder, helping me up and out into the light of day. The brightness was like a brand on my eyelids. I squinted, praying for my eyes to adjust.

"Are ye feeling any better?" she asked. A strange listlessness filled me.

"The ache in my head has gone, but I'm weak an' tired still." We sat in the courtyard under a bright, cold sky. Perched as high as we were, the land was like one vast green carpet that stretched over hills and rolled on forever. The colors were crisp and vibrant, and everything had a sharp edge I didn't remember before.

Where the camp of the Bruce had been, we saw no trace. Way off in the distance glistened the blue water of several lochs that dotted the landscape. Looking down I was reminded of the map that began the whole of my journey and changed my life.

"Which way is home?" I asked aloud.

"There, I would think." She pointed toward the east.

"Why?" I wasn't really questioning her statement as much as wondering how she made the judgment. I had no idea of my own.

"I heard once that there is a string o' lochs in the Highlands that resembles the shape o' a horse. There ye can see the head, an' over there the backbone. The tail points toward the ocean."

I stood, marveling for a moment, and then noticed a ripple of mirth that swam across the surface of her mind. "Yer having me on!"

Her giggle broke, unhindered. "Aye. I don't have any idea which way we should go." Her laughter loosened the tension within me and I smiled. "Seems as good a way as any." She got up and brought back my pack. "There's no' a whole lot o' food left. I had to feed the horse a bit an' there's no' much to forage up here."

I ate a raw potato. It tasted old and flat, and did little to fill the hole inside me. There were only fish and sparse vegetables in the sack. The rapid beat of a heart flit across my mind, and I turned automatically in the direction of it. A large hare darted through a hole in the wall.

"Dinner." I got to my feet, dizzy with the movement, but Aine held me back. "Wait." Softly she began to hum, and from my sensing of him I felt the rabbit stop. She nodded in its direction and I went after it. I was no stranger to catching and killing animals in the wild, but this seemed different. My stomach grumbled then, and I quickly grabbed it by the neck and twisted hard and fast. *Never let an animal suffer needlessly.* My da's words echoed in my mind, but oddly enough the image of the Templar hung before me.

Then the place around me changed. Dark. Cold, hard-packed earth. Men all around, broken and bleeding.

"Confess and all your sins will be absolved."

A man's sobbing cut the air and whispers rustled. *"Innocent. I am innocent!"*

A shiver rippled through me as Aine took the rabbit from my limp fingers. "Come. Ye do too much, too soon."

We built a new fire outside in a bare patch of earth. Aine was adamant that she wouldn't go back inside the broch. I wasn't sure how I felt about it, or about anything. I skinned and cleaned the rabbit listlessly, and Aine skewered the meat on thin sticks she'd cleaned. She laid them in the fire. I stared at the flames, the smell of the meat making my stomach roll. I forced myself to look away.

She turned the skewers and the meat sizzled and popped. The sound, the smell. I barely made it to my knees and crawled a little away before I was sick. There was nothing in me, but it didn't stop the retching.

I felt Aine's hand on my back and the song in the air. My heaves slowed. "I know it's the last thing ye want to do, but ye have to eat."

My stomach clenched at the thought. "Not the meat. You take that. I need to settle. Another potato."

She nodded. "I'll save some for later."

I didn't know how to tell her that I might never be able to eat it. For some reason it triggered memories of a vision I had tried to forget. I saw the Grand Master,

Jacques de Molay, burned at the stake. The image had been uppermost in the string of dreams I'd had below.

I rested awhile and Aine saw to the horse. Part of me wanted to just lie down and let whatever was to come take me, but the other part knew I couldn't. "Should we stay another day or move on?" she asked.

"We have to leave here." I stood, but my legs were trembling. "Let's move on as soon as we can."

"Ye'll get no argument from me," she replied, readying the horse. I put out the fire and hefted our pack, nearly dropping it again. My arms were so weak I could hardly carry it.

"Ready?" she asked.

I nodded and followed her and the horse. When we were just beyond the outer wall, I looked back at the great stone fort. I had something to do here, but it was not something I was equipped or ready for just yet.

PART TWO

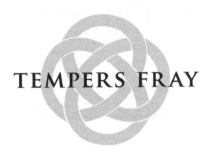

TEMPERS FRAY

We rode for long stretches, and walked for short, then did it again and again. The horse was strong and chosen well for travel, but we were two passengers to the one and our burden was much.

Late in the afternoon of the second day, we stopped to eat the last of the food in my pack. Down to two small onions and a dried-up bit of herring that we ate cold. My stomach was protesting and I was feeling the lack.

"Tormod, ye don't look well," Aine said, watching me from across the small fire we had built.

"Well, how am I supposed to look? Every part of me pains, we're lost, an' out o' food," I snapped at her without a moment's thought or hesitation. Surprise and hurt whipped through her to me.

"An' why am I to blame for all o' this?" Her voice was low and lethal.

"Well, I didn't eat all the food," I said beneath my breath. I knew even as it left my mouth that I was not being fair.

"No, ye didn't. Ye took a little lay-down an' left me to do everything to keep ye alive!" Her eyes flashed and her fists curled. "If I knew ye'd be such a beast, I'd no' have wasted my time."

"Oh, really?" Irritation was quickly turning to something worse.

"Oooooo, ye make me so mad!" she snarled, readying for the confrontation that escalated between us from nowhere.

"Go on then, just try it. I've a mind to turn ye over a tree stump and wallop ye for the first time ye slugged me!"

Aine launched herself at me. I had just enough mind to turn my face away before her fists rained down. And just as quickly, I wrapped my arms tight around her, pinning her own down by her sides. "Ye let me go, Tormod MacLeod, or I'll knee ye so bad ye won't stand for days!"

"Someone should have taught ye manners by now, Aine Cleary. An' I've a mind to do it!"

Her eyes were blazing and my temper was burning hotter than I'd ever felt. I didn't know where mine ended and hers began. It was as if the emotion bounced between the two of us with nothing to bank or dispel it and so it grew and raged.

Aine twisted in my arms, trying to maim me with her knees, and I struggled, determined to turn her aside and give her the beating she deserved, when in the burst of a heartbeat my world went black.

Aine sat on a high rock, her knees drawn up before her, her eyes red from crying. Her fear and hurt wafted through me as did the thoughts at the edge of her mind. She thought me like him, William, the man who raised his fists to her with little provocation. She blamed herself.

I was flat out on my back, and the brightness of the day burned the backs of my eyes. "What happened?"

"Tormod, I fear there's something grievously wrong with ye." Her voice was nothing like the Aine of a moment ago. She was timid and worried.

Memory came at me in a rush. "Lord, did I hurt ye?" I raked my mind, praying nothing had come of our argument.

"No. Ye fainted before we got anywhere." The relief I felt at her words made me light-headed. "But that was no' right." She didn't make to move any nearer me. "I've been sitting here thinking about what happened, an' though I know I was to blame as much as ye, something more is at work. If ye think on it, there was truly nothing so disastrous happening to either one of us that would have warranted that attack."

I knew what she meant and agreed. But it had happened, reason or not. "Did ye come to any conclusions?" I asked, struggling to sit.

"Aye. I don't know how, but ye know the way ye can feel the emotions o' others?"

"Aye." It was my greatest problem at the moment. I felt her terror of me. It was making me sick with disgust.

"Well, I think, between us, it's no' just that ye feel what I feel. I think ye feel it, an' it grows inside ye, then I feel it, an' it grows in me. An' on to ye again, until it's so mean ye have to pass out before yer body overloads an' allows ye to do something ye wouldn't normally."

That was exactly it, like it was all growing and multiplying and spreading like a bad vine. "Aye. Ye could be right. I don't know what we can do about it, though. We're kind o' stuck with each other for the time being." I don't know why I put it to her that way. It hurt her and I felt a beast for it.

She took a deep breath as if calming herself. "I think now that we know what can happen, we just have to watch ourselves. An' when we start feeling out o' control, we have to try an' break the hold. I don't know how. Get away. Jump in a stream if we have to." She shivered and I felt a darkness slip from her mind to mine. "Ye wanted to kill me, Tormod. I've felt it before." Memories of her uncle flitted through her mind.

"I'm no' him, Aine. I'd never hurt ye if I could help it." I met her eyes, willing her to believe.

Aine got down from her perch slowly and came to my side. She was frightened, but determined to get over it. I felt the courage she was gathering and did my best to make sure my emotions were in check and my thoughts calm.

She knelt down by my side, with wide uncertain eyes. Then slowly, as if in a dream, she leaned toward me. I stayed very still. Slowly she shifted closer, until her body was so near to mine that I took in her breath.

"I'm sorry, Aine," I said softly, lifting my hands to her shoulders. She was suddenly shy, looking down at my chest, and a flutter of uncertainty passed between us. "Look at me," I said. "Deeply, horribly sorry that I acted that way." Purposely I called on a tendril of power and opened my mind wide to her, showing exactly how ashamed I was of my behavior. Her eyes went wide with surprise. And in that moment I moved the small distance between us and kissed her.

UNEXPECTED ENCOUNTER

I hadn't meant to. It just sort of happened. I'd never kissed a lass before, but it didn't seem to be something one could do wrong. Her lips were soft and warm, and she smelled of wood smoke and harvest. I didn't know if she had done any kissing before this, but she seemed fair good at it. My head was spinning and the world around was bright and filled with heat.

"Ahem." The sound went off like a shout in my brain. I scrambled back, pushing Aine away. She gasped with a flare of anger.

An enormous gray hound bounded into the clearing, barking and circling us. His master was our mysterious speaker. He stood nearly six hands for sure, with a stout frame, bushy black beard, and piercing blue eyes. "What have we here, Bran? Two visitors to our lonely land. What am I to make o' this?"

I helped Aine to her feet, palming my dagger as she shielded his view of my body. He didn't look or sound a threat, but then I was no fair judge at the moment. The man came close, nearly within sniffing distance. I was at once affronted, for he eyed Aine as if he'd not seen one of her kind for many a year. I was getting annoyed that men continually seemed obsessed by her.

"Who are ye, an' what d'ye mean, riling up my dog?" He had the look of someone unhinged, and made sharp, quick movements.

"Just travelers, lost on our way, sir. We mean ye no harm or disrespect."

"Travelers?" he nearly shouted. "Travelers, ye say. Who but a spirit would travel here at the turn o' the season?"

"We got lost on our way. We were meant to arrive at my brother's long ago." The lie tripped from my lips with little help from me at all.

"Hmmf," he said, and I couldn't tell if he believed me or not. "We don't see much company, Bran an' I. Come along, then. Ye look as if a good meal would no' go amiss."

His whistle cut the air and the dog immediately pulled from Aine, who he had been sniffing. His eyes darted from his master to her, seemingly torn as to who he wanted to stay with.

"Follow me. My hut's near. We'll set ye to right an' ye can tell me what goes on in the world."

It seemed the best of ideas. Aine and I still didn't know which way was out. I grabbed her hand and sent a mental feel of caution her way. Immediately my head began to swim and pound.

"Don't do it," she whispered harshly. "Avoid the power."

I knew it, even at the time, but it did me no good. My reaching and pulling was second nature. I had to stop, though, and start paying attention. The nausea was already on me, and I was having trouble seeing through a fog that lightened and darkened as we walked.

We followed the bounding leaps of Bran and the great stride of his master out of the clearing, up and down several wooded slopes, and finally to the door of a hut that was surrounded by great beech trees.

This was where all similarity to what I had expected ended. Beyond the door was a direct contrast to the hard-edged mountain man we had met. Something hot and fragrant simmered over an enormous fire in the hearth. Spices wafted and herbs hung from the edges of the roof beam. A brilliant tapestry draped one full wall, and all around the space artistry was gathered. Pottery. Carvings. More tapestries. Golden statues and real books. The artful clutter decorated every available surface. Even an ornamented table, very much like one I had seen in the castle of Dover, stood in an alcove that you wouldn't have known was there from the outside.

On the table were parchment and quill, and some-one — I had such trouble reconciling the mountain man with the idea of this someone — had been crafting a journal entry some time before. Aine stared around her with a look of awe.

"Come in. Aye. Come in. Bran an' I have no' had company in a dog's age. Ha!" He shouted and laughed at nearly the same time. "A dog's age!"

I found myself perplexed by this large, loud man, but met his grin. He seemed to have about him a joy in living that was hard to suppress and oddly contagious.

"Hungry? I've the best venison stew in all the countryside," he said.

"Aye. Fair starved," said Aine, preventing any comment from me at all. This whole visit had me at odds. He was a strange sort.

"Sit ye down, then." His voice was almost too loud in the space. After the broch and the quiet of the road, I was unnerved.

Aine had moved from my grasp to peel off her cloak, and the dizziness came on me twofold. "Is that sage I smell?" she asked, oblivious to my discomfort.

"Och, aye. Ye've a nose for the spices, lass?"

"My mam was a fiend for drying them, an' then dousing the food," she replied.

"Dousing! Good Lord in heaven, lass. There'll be no dousing in the home o' Cornelius MacTavish. Chefs to the Laird o' the Isles we are. Skilled as sages in the art of fine eating. We were, anyway." He poured off the steaming, fragrant mix and my stomach rumbled. I took a stool by a table large enough to fit three comfortably and rested a moment, letting the sounds and smells roll over me, trying to settle my queasiness.

Bran hovered near Aine, his big brown gaze following her every movement, as did his owner. I couldn't put a finger on why the man stared until his words made it clear.

"Lord, lass, ye 'mind me o' my daughter." This time the words were said at a much more ear-friendly level, a pure whisper from this man. Loss and pain swirled around me. Aine moved quickly to my side and, as she dropped to the stool nearest, brushed my knees with her own. She had known, then. The respite gave me time to lock down what was left of my thin inner shielding.

"What happened to her?" Aine asked.

"Went home to the angels an' her blessed mother, near on a year ago. Ye gave us a bit o' a fright when ye appeared out o' nowhere. Bran here is still wambly. He knows yer no' Catriona, but he's reminded as am I."

I wondered how he knew what the dog was thinking. Bran ambled over and lay at Aine's feet, never taking his eyes from her. I thought perhaps he was right. Mayhap it was living alone together that gave him the edge.

Cornelius stooped at a low trunk set against the wall and drew out a small portrait. It was as skillfully done as the ones I'd seen on the walls of Dover castle, and the likeness to Aine was there in the hair and shape of the face.

"Where are ye from, lass?" he asked.

"My folk are from Eire, originally around County Cork. But I don't remember any o' it. I was only three when we moved to Scotia."

"An' where be they now, that yer wandering about the world with yon rascal?" I didn't like his description of me — or his interest in Aine.

Her face fell and I felt the sudden surge of sadness hit her. I reached for her knee to comfort her and the sadness raised a notch. I pulled away as if I'd been scalded. Cornelius didn't seem to notice. "They've passed on with the rest o' my family," Aine said, barely containing the grief inside her.

"I'm sorry, lass. I didn't mean to bring ye pain." Aine looked down at her bowl, the sadness slipping back and forth between us. "Never ye mind, never ye mind. Ye're both welcome here for as long as ye need." He smiled at her with a fondness I thought a bit misplaced. He didn't, after all, know Aine. Perhaps it was missing his daughter and wife that brought it on. He shrugged then and it was as if his whole body got into the act. "Och, well. Enough o' the old an' on to the new. What brings ye out into the middle o' nowhere?"

I answered as Aine seemed transfixed by her food. "We were traveling to meet family in —"

"Actually," Aine broke in, "we seek a healer by the name o' Beaton. He was along with the men o' Robert the Bruce until quite recently. D'ye know the man?" She turned and looked directly at Cornelius. I was shocked and no little bit furious with her for not sticking to our story and for telling a stranger that we had been with the Bruce when he was no doubt going to be looking for us.

"Aye. Bertrand is a friend. There's no' much diversion in this bit o' the world, nor safe haven when ye're out an' about with nowhere to lay yer head. Bertrand has a gift with the herbs. We are of a kind."

"An' when did ye see Bertrand last?" I asked.

"Och, no' for quite some time. Months," he said. No help at all to us. He hadn't come this way.

"We've lost our bearings in these mountains, Cornelius. D'ye think ye an' Bran could show us the way out o' here?" Aine asked.

"Aye, o' course. But take yer time. Eat an' rest here the night," he said.

Aine and I shared a look and I asked, "D'ye think we could buy a bit o' supplies before we leave? We've used all we came with."

"There'll be no talk o' payment!" he nearly bellowed, taking me by surprise. " 'Tis no' the Highland way!"

"No offense meant to ye, sir," I stammered. "We didn't want to abuse yer hospitality." He was an excitable one. My inners were jumpy, with so very many emotions and explosions in so short a span of time.

"I'll fix ye up a parcel o' food. We've got more than enough for Bran an' I to go two winters." Bran's head lifted the moment his master mentioned his name, his ears pricking with interest. "Lass, if yon pack is all ye have in the way o' clothing, help yerself to Catriona's. I could no' bring myself to get rid o' it. Good that someone uses it."

I tucked into the stew that had lain neglected in my bowl while we spoke. Its flavors were strong on my tongue and welcome. Aine seemed to come to and took a mouthful sopped up by a bannock. "Lord, man, this is a bit o' heaven." She smiled at me and I returned it.

"Thank ye for the compliment." Cornelius gave a courtly bow that, at the same time was out of character, looked right on him as well, then crossed to a large wardrobe that stood in a corner.

"How d'ye know to bow that way?" I asked. "If I did it I'd tip over on my nose."

"Years o' practice, laddie. My travels have taken me to many an odd place, to be sure."

"This is wonderful," Aine beamed, nodding toward her bowl. "How did ye do it?"

"Family secret, lass. An' unless ye want to marry Bran or I, we can't give it up." His teasing brought light to her eyes and reminded me of how few times I'd seen her smile since we'd met. Still, to have someone else make her smile tightened my guts.

Her happiness slid around inside me, and for some reason I remembered our kiss. Aine looked up at that moment and I felt my face go hot.

HAVEN

Throughout the early hours of evening, Bran followed Aine wherever she went: to the cupboard where Catriona's clothing was kept, to the outhouse where he sat dutifully while she did what was necessary, into the root cellar where Cornelius stored grain and vegetables, and back to the house where, behind a screen, she put on the dead girl's clothes.

"Tor, look!" She'd never used my shortened name before and I was just enjoying the soft way she said it, when she stepped from behind the screen. Of a sudden my tongue felt too big for my mouth. She was lovely.

The whole of the dress was pale green, and embroidered flowers of pink and yellow dotted the top. Boldly, she lifted her skirts and showed me fine stockings striped yellow and green. Cornelius had been outside and came in as she was dancing about. His smile was pleased and sad at the same time.

"She was much like ye, lass. Lit up a room the moment she smiled."

I'd never noticed it before, but now that he mentioned it I saw that it was true. I smiled at her and when she returned the smile, a faint pink tinged the usual white of her skin.

"There's a kertch an' apron there as well. Take them. They're yers."

She drew them out and tucked her hair into a bit of material that matched the skirt. "They're lovely," she said. "Are ye sure? I've never had anything half so wonderful."

"Aye, lass. It clashes with my beard." He grinned and hefted a pack heavily onto the table. "Just a few more things."

"That's for us?" I asked, astounded. "But ye don't even know us!"

He met my eyes squarely. "I know good when I see it. It's just Highland hospitality, as I said before. At the moment I've more than enough. It's only right to share." A look of concern crossed Cornelius's face just then. "Tormod, yer looking a bit on the peaked side."

"I'm all right." Thankfully nothing had gone amiss since we'd been here.

"Well, lay in for a good night's rest and maybe a bit o' yer color will return."

Nothing sounded better. As we sat around the fire, my eyes had begun to drag downward. I had my plaid tucked up around my ears, and Cornelius had given us each a warm blanket. The hut was not immune to the cold wind whipping beyond the stone of its walls, but the fire did much to heat the place.

"Ye're both fit to drop. Why don't ye go on, then? Ye can have the trundle, lass. 'Twas Catriona's. Tormod, there's a second pallet in my room ye're welcome to."

My body stiffened. I had not spent a night without contact from Aine since I'd met her. Her worry slid through my mind as strong as my own. "If ye don't mind, I'll just lay down here, near the fire," I said.

Cornelius's look passed over me then. "Tormod, what are yer intentions toward yonder lass?"

The question startled me. "What?"

"Well, it's no' proper to be roaming about together, alone or unattended. I ask o' yer intentions." He was not my da, but he was somebody's da, and he had taken a fatherly attitude toward Aine.

"I have no intentions at all toward her," I sputtered. Aine looked over quickly, her face dipping toward red, but instead of her usual threat of curled knuckles, she turned ahead again and only a stiff back and swirl of hurt gave any hint of her thoughts. I hurried to explain. "I'm to be a Knight Templar. The Order is chaste."

"Still," he prodded, "ye're not a knight as yet." He was obviously remembering the kiss and wondering, no doubt, if I should be left alone in the room with her. My face flamed. "I ask if ye're honorable."

It was embarrassing to have to defend my character. "I am. I've no untoward thought o' the lass. I've no thoughts about her one way or another." In my bumbling manner I was far from gracious. Aine's jolt of anger ripped through my senses and I had to hold my head to keep it from tumbling from my body. Still, she did not turn around. Why was she so angry? I hadn't said anything bad. This was all too much. I felt so horrid, it made no sense. I just wanted to sleep beside her. My breath was growing short and my eyes were starting to blur. Lord, no! Not here!

Riders raced away along the shore. Flames filled the night sky. Our boat was engulfed. Da and his men rushed the waves but it was too late.

Da! I shouted, trying to reach him.

The world lurched. Aine was crouched over me, and her anger had turned to fear. Her hands were on my chest, but it did little to ease my agitation. She did not hum, I knew, because Cornelius was there. "We have to leave," I said urgently.

"Lad, ye need to rest," said Cornelius. "Ye're in a bad way."

I had to speak to Aine, make her understand. I sent a small push. *Aine*, I tried.

"Tormod," she gasped, "ye know ye can't do that!"

Heat slammed my mind, shutting out everything but the pain in my temples. I cried out as the sudden jags ripped through me.

"Lass, I'm worried." Cornelius's face was a mask of concern. "This is beyond the skills of the folk here about."

"We have to find this Beaton," Aine said. "D'ye have any idea where he might be?"

I could hear them speaking but my mind would not calm. The wind blew hard in my ears. The earth pressed solid at my back. Another vision was coming. Lord, no. I couldn't take any more.

A gown of silken blue. Cloak of white. Curls tucked tight in a braided crown around her head. Aine's hand in the crook of Cornelius's arm.

"Tormod! Please listen to me. Ye must let it go." Aine was beside herself. I felt the weight of her body and the despair in her heart. I was back. I could move.

"I'm all right, Aine." I rested my hand on the back of her head. I was as weak as a newborn. "I have to go home. Right away," I said, barely able to speak.

"We will, Tormod. Tomorrow. Cornelius will lead us toward the shore," she said. "Ye scared the very devil out o' me. I don't know how much more either o' us can take." She looked up, her eyes glistening and red. Cornelius was beside her, and Bran took the moment to lick her cheeks. She laughed and pushed him away. "I'm no' the one who is ill, Bran." She squeezed me tight. "Tormod, promise me ye'll stop."

I knew she meant using the power, but Cornelius didn't. "Lass, he's no' well. He canno' keep himself from the attack."

I needed to get Aine alone to tell her what I'd seen. I could no longer think only of myself. I'd brought the trouble home, and left my family to fend for themselves. It was folly to have run in the first place, but what of the vision of Aine? She was with Cornelius. Did that mean I should leave her behind?

She sat up and the break in contact made the bile roil in my gut. No, not yet. I couldn't give her up yet. I reached for her hand, and she helped me over to the pallet. Her touch righted my world once again.

"I'll just sleep a bit now, if ye don't mind," I murmured. Aine sat by my side with her hand on my arm. Her touch helped and I let myself drift. It was the last I knew of the day.

THE PATH HOME

"I hate to leave ye this way," Cornelius said as we crested a rise overlooking the start of a long road back toward the sea. We had been traveling much of the morning.

"We'll be all right. Thank ye, Cornelius. Ye've done so much for us," Aine said.

From where we sat on the horse I could see for leagues. Cornelius reached inside his surcoat and drew something small from his pocket. "Take this and follow it east and south." He held a small compass set in a golden locket. "D'ye know how to use one?"

"I do," I said. "It's no' difficult. Ye just lay it flat in yer palm an' watch where the needle points. It will always want to go north, so if ye're walking in the wrong direction ye can correct yerself." I began to lift my hand for it, but Cornelius dropped its chain over Aine's head.

"Stay safe, both o' ye, till we meet again."

Aine clutched the locket and nodded as he turned away. I found myself a little put off that he hadn't given the compass to me, but Aine held it as if it were her only possession, so I didn't bother to say anything.

Bran was not as easy to part with as his master. He bounded after us, torn between coming and going. "Go on, lad. We'll see ye again," Aine said as he continued to follow our horse.

"He'll go back on his own soon enough," I said. I knew the pull of his master would win out over the draw of us.

"Yer sure? I don't want him to get lost in these woods." At his master's whistle he bounded away and we didn't see him again. The sudden silence was astounding. I hadn't realized that Cornelius was giving off as much emotion as he must have.

"Are ye sure ye're no' feeling faint?" Aine asked. I stared at the back of her head wondering if she had asked me that before. We'd been riding but I had no idea how long. When I didn't answer she urged the horse to stop.

A wide burn trickled downhill. We'd been following it. I remembered the water and the look of it moving over the land. Her hand moved along my chest. "Tor, yer sark is soaked clear through an' yer face an' hair are wet as well." She jumped down and helped me off. Aine's hands were on my face. They were as cold as I was hot, and I flinched.

"Ye're burning up. I don't like this. Take off yer boots an' get yer feet into the water."

My hands plucked at my boots, but I couldn't make them do what I wanted. I frowned at them.

Aine pressed the water skin to my mouth and pulled off the boots. I felt her flush of surprise at my missing toes, and I buried them under the silt. Wet cloth wiped my face, and I closed my eyes and lay back on a scattering of dry needles that covered the ground. Water trickled over my forehead, and then again I felt the wipe of the cloth.

"We've got to bring yer body heat down." She seemed to be talking to herself. The shape of her was dark and the edges light. "Ye're getting worse," she said, agitated. "You've got to stop the visions from coming. There has to be a way."

"Best o' luck with that. I've never been able to control them before, what makes ye think I can now?"

"I don't know but we're no' going to make it back to warn yer da if we don't find a way." As hot as I was, her words brought a chill rippling through me and my skin rose with gooseflesh.

"Cold now?" she asked. I didn't answer, just closed my eyes and thought for a bit. Aine was right. It was getting worse. I was losing track of time. Memories mixed with visions, and I could not tell them apart. Panic gnawed inside me. Aine was able to take the edge off the worst of it, but inside I felt like I was being torn in two.

Aine's hum was strong, loud, and unworried. She seemed at ease with no one to remark on her strange behavior. Still, I slid away.

The room was lit by many candles, and yet the darkness was so thick I could taste it. Men were gathered around a long table. The white of the cloth covering it glowed bright.

"We must get inside. Something is happening. Rumors have begun."

"They know nothing. How could they?"

Several voices sought to be heard.

"They know of the carving and bowl. The boy unleashed its power before them."

"An unfortunate event."

The voices were all but one strange to me, and yet even the one was murky. I knew not who the speaker was.

"We must infiltrate the court as well as the residence. We must know the meaning behind the request."

"He knows that we are not to be trifled with." This voice was younger and brasher than the rest.

"Do not assume that the Order is all powerful. Even the greatest may be reduced to nothing with the smallest of stones."

"Tormod!" Aine's voice cut through the most illuminating vision I had yet to receive. I tried to ignore her and call it back to me, but she shook me and damped my sight.

"I need to see." I pulled away from her touch and instantly regretted it. The world heaved around me, and she reached once again to give me peace. "Hellfires, Aine! Let go! I have to see." I didn't realize that I was shouting until I saw and felt the fear in her.

"Ye're killing yerself, Tormod. Ye have to stop." Without warning, thoughts of the bairn and what I had done to him came back and slammed my mind. In my state of agitation, I had advanced on her with menace, leaning over her as if to strike. She was frightened of me, and for me. "I'm sorry," she whimpered. "I'm only trying to help."

I reached for her and she only barely allowed my touch. "I'm sorry, Aine. I'm shattering inside, and yet each episode brings me closer to understanding what is going on beyond."

"Beyond what, or where?" she asked, near tears. "None of this makes any sense."

I sat down heavily. "Aye. It doesn't."

I was burning and lost. Everything within and without ached. I buried my face in my arms as the world pulsed around me.

LOST

It was dark and the wood was lit by a small fire. Aine was by my side, wiping my face and neck with a cool cloth. "Glad ye decided to join me," she said when she noticed I had awakened. She was quietly spent. Exhaustion hung about her like a woolen cloak.

I lifted my hand to her pale cheek, shocked by how much it trembled on its way. She leaned into it. "How d'ye feel?" she asked. Her eyes shone in the firelight.

"Like I've been running, even in my dreams, forever," I said. The pounding in my head had eased and I didn't feel hot anymore, but my clothes felt damp and uncomfortable.

"The burning seems to have passed. Ye've sweated it out."

"I feel like it." I sat up slowly, peeling the sark away from my chest with a grimace.

"Ye've other clothes in the pack. D'ye want me to fetch them?" She was speaking softly, moving slowly. I nodded.

I climbed to my feet and steadied myself against a tree limb, dizzy with the effort. I tried to pull off my sark, but my arms were useless. "Here, let me," she said, already back. Her hands brushed my sides as she lifted the tunic over my head, and the skin tingled where she touched. I felt a rush of color fill my face.

As she handed me the fresh sark, a trickle of uncertainty flickered through her. "Shall I help? Or can ye manage?"

"I can do it," I said, not at all sure. "I'm sorry, Aine," I said. "I had no right to snap at ye. I feel terrible."

"I know. Leave it be. Stay calm. It's taken me much to get ye there." Her voice was hoarse.

I had shouted at her. I nearly hit her. *What kind of monster was I becoming?* I thought with self-loathing.

"Tormod, stop," Aine gasped. "Yer emotions are rubbing me raw." Her eyes had filled with tears.

And then I saw her. Pale and still, with blood seeping from the back of her head. My hands. Red.

I jerked as if I'd been stabbed, the world spinning. I stared at her with horror. What did this mean? "I'd never hurt ye, Aine! Never." Hysteria was building and I couldn't tamp it down.

She dropped down beside me and grabbed my shoulders. "I know, Tormod. Calm ye now."

She hadn't seen what I had. I could barely face her. The terrible vision still hung vibrantly in my mind's eye. *What I see happens.* The thought was terrifying.

"Look at me," she demanded. "Ye didn't," she said. "An' ye won't." She stared at me, willing me to accept what she was insisting, but how could I? I had seen it.

Then without a word she tilted her head and pressed her lips to mine. All at once it was as if the world grew still. Nothing mattered but the feel of her in my arms and the taste of her mouth. Nothing I could ever remember felt as good or right. We kissed for a time that seemed to stretch on forever. With no one watching or caring or stopping us, with the power of the land flowing around and through us, it was as if we had become one person. My head was clear and my body alive.

Aine was the first to break off, pushing me away when I would have gone on for days. Our breathing was quick, and a feel of uncertainty wafted between us. "We should, ye should," she stammered, "clean up. Finish." Her words were jumbled, stumbling over one another in confusion as she shoved the sark I'd dropped back into my hands. She was away, back by the fire before I knew what had happened.

What had happened? I wondered as I washed in the burn and she tended the fire and the fish from Cornelius. *She had wanted me to kiss her, hadn't she? She had started*

it. I was no clearer by the time I'd finished and made my way to the fire.

I would have tried to read her thoughts, but I was sorely afraid to use the power. I was sensing odd, mixed feelings from her. Happiness. Discomfort. It was as if she couldn't decide what she felt. I tried to seal her feelings off from me, but we were sharing whether we liked it or not.

"Here. Eat." Again the awkward, choppy words.

I took the fish, wondering if maybe I shouldn't have kissed her at all. If this was the way we would be with each other, maybe it would be best if I never did again. I watched her beneath my lids. "Did ye get any sleep?"

Aine looked fit to drop. She had been pulling on the power to keep me from crashing so much lately, and I'd only now thought about what it cost her. She had barely eaten and her eyes were drooping. "No. There hasn't been time."

"I'll watch over ye now," I said, moving near and stretching out on my side, assuming she would lie with me. Instead, she curled up a short way from me, closer to the fire. When had she ever done that? Lasses were confusing. I lay there long, wondering if I should move closer. I could use her peace, but I wasn't altogether sure she was peaceful at all. In moments she was asleep.

"Aine?" I said softly.

Only her rattle of breath met my query. My mind was still on edge and my body shivery, shaking. Quietly and slowly, I moved myself closer. She didn't acknowledge my approach so I turned back-to-back and leaned against her. Calm immediately enfolded me and I felt a bit guilty. I hoped that she wouldn't mind.

COLD COMFORT

We traveled hard the next day, moving over land that dipped and swelled like the waves of the ocean. We were bone tired, and the oddness was still hanging between us.

I said my prayers as we journeyed, and the carving was much in my thoughts. I missed it. When I carried it, I always felt as if I were being looked after, as if somehow the Lady was my protector instead of the other way around. Out here I was alone. Not truly alone, as I had Aine with me, but it wasn't the same.

"Tormod, look," she said, shaking me from my thoughts. I shielded my eyes from the glare of the sun and saw the twist of smoke from a cook fire. It was coming from a village up ahead. I could feel the presence of people scattered among the huts. As we rode closer, we saw one dwelling larger than the others. "It has an inn. Let's stay the night." Her voice had a pleading edge that I knew and felt.

"If we can," I said. "I can't be around people right now, so let's hope there aren't many."

The inn was large, old, and dark. A couple of stools flanked the door, and one enormous table filled much of the space. On either side were long, low benches and I dropped to the closest one, unable to do more. A low fire burned in the hearth, its dull glow nearly the only break in the dimness. There was a door at the far side of the room, and from beyond we heard the rattle of salvers being stacked.

"Where is everyone?" Aine asked uneasily.

"I don't know, but the quiet is welcome."

A small, thin man stepped from behind a curtain near the back. His lank hair hung in greasy strands and his clothes were baggy and dirty. "Looking for a room?" His eyes darted from Aine to me and back again.

"Aye," I said, "an' a bite to eat." My head swam with the feel of the man. He was like a hungry rat, ready to attack.

"Ye've come at a good time. We were fair burstin' a' the seams just a day gone by." My body tensed.

"Oh? Why was that?" It was hard for me to speak. My mind already felt raw and the man's foulness was making it worse.

"Men o' the northern clans were in, looking to find Robert the Bruce," he said. Aine's bristle of wariness hit me like a blow. My own was strong enough to make me weak.

"Is the Bruce in this bit o' the land?"

"He was, awhile back, but moved on," he said.

I knew it was not my imagination then that the man took that moment to look me over. His sharp gaze was calculating. I felt Aine shift beside me. She had noticed it as well.

"How much for a night and meal?" We would be gone long before morning, but it was important the innkeeper did not know that.

"Two coppers," he said.

I paid him from Torquil's money, feeling badly that it would be a waste.

"Have a seat an' the mistress will be in to serve ye." There was something in the way he said it that made the skin at my neck crawl. Aine edged her way to the table and we exchanged a look behind the man's retreating back. I nodded toward the door.

I was dead on my feet and starving, but the man had mischief on his mind. I couldn't read much, but Aine's tight grip on my hand said she agreed. We slipped through the doors and out into the woods, leading the horse so as not to alert the owner of the inn.

We moved quickly and silently until we were a good way off, then mounted. "They've been tracking ye since Arbroath, an' they're getting help from the local magistrate. There is a warrant out for both o' us for murder."

My breath seized. "Ye read the room?"

"Aye. They offered him money for information about us. We have to get somewhere safe an' find a way to change our looks," said Aine.

The woods around me faded suddenly, and I felt myself begin to slump on the horse as light burst all around.

"If you manage this feat, you will be the most powerful ruler in all the world."

"God is beside me always. I am his most treasured chosen. It will be."

Aine's arms were around me and her grip was fierce. "Tormod, stay with me!" As the woods came back into focus, I could feel her shaking me.

"More is happening," I murmured. "Much more than any o' us knows." Aine looked at me askance and I answered before she could ask. "King Philippe is planning something. The evidence is all there in my visions, if only I could put the pieces together."

"It's no' our concern right now. We can only worry about staying out o' the hands o' the soldiers an' keeping yer mind intact." She began to hum, and the pull of the vision faded. "We've no time to spare," she said when she finished.

The rest of the day passed in a blur of leagues and trees. We pressed the horse to travel longer at a canter, walked less, and only stopped when it was too dark to maneuver safely. We needed time and space between them and us.

AS ONE

"We have to stop," Aine said finally. We'd come to the summit of yet another hill, following the path of a burn that snaked across the landscape, and darkness was approaching fast.

"We put distance between us today, but they'll make it back if they find our tracks," I said. Though we'd crossed a good deal of country and taken the horse through several burns to remove our scent, we had moved too quickly to be truly careful.

The land before me tilted and my stomach wrenched. "It doesn't matter. I can go no farther." I slid from the horse, gripping my stomach so it wouldn't heave.

"I don't know how ye've made it this far. I am ready to drop," she said, groaning.

The trees around me swayed and I with them. I sat down heavily, my breath short.

"Here." Aine passed the water skin into my hands, and gave me a bannock to settle my stomach. The water was warm, but it helped. She pressed an apple on me a few moments later, but as I focused on her outstretched hand, my sight seemed to fade in and out.

"Tormod . . ." she said hesitantly. I felt her hands on my head but suddenly couldn't see her face.

"Aine!" I was blind, and panic whipped through me. "I can't see. What's happening?!" I heard Aine's hum, but it seemed to do nothing to clear the darkness.

This vision was comprised only of sound.

"What do ye mean we've missed them?!" The hiss of Gaylen's voice made me tremble. *"Where were they headed? In which direction did they travel?"*

I felt Aine beside me and heard her swift intake of breath.

"I don't know, truly. I'd no' thought they would leave. They paid for food an' a room. I came to find ye straightaway. My mistress was preparing the meal with something that would delay them."

The conversation cut off suddenly, and oddly there was hardly any of the residual backlash from the vision. The clearing came sharply back into focus, and I realized

Aine was crouched in front of me with a stunned expression on her face. "What?" I asked.

"I've never done that before," she said as if to herself.

"Done what?" I asked. I was still struggling to understand what had happened.

"I joined yer vision," she said. "I read it like a place I'd come upon. I saw Gaylen and heard him question the innkeeper. He's after us as well," she said, sighing. Then with little warning she swayed and sat heavily on her backside. I reached to steady her in case she went farther toward the ground.

"Are ye all right?"

She nodded.

"But I don't understand. I only heard the vision. Ye saw and heard it as well?" I asked. No mistake, this was a strange new turn of events.

"Aye, an' I feel all wambly now. Not bad, but a bit weak an' shaky," she said.

"An' I feel a million times better than when I usually have a vision," I said, trying to puzzle it out.

"Well, that's our answer then. We've found a way to get ye through this. Ye can't stop the visions from coming, but if I can get to ye at their outset, I can take the burden from ye." We stared at each other, amazed by the thought of it. "We can get ye home, Tormod. Well, if we can manage to avoid the many factions hunting us."

Even without a severe response to the vision, my head was drooping. I could barely focus on the rest of her words. Aine, however, recovered in only moments. She was up and pacing and thinking aloud. "I knew that we were meant to work together. I just didn't know how." She turned to me. "The question now is, how can we use this to our advantage?"

"You figure it out. I have to take a little rest." I closed my eyes and listened to the sound of twigs snapping as she continued to wear a footpath in the clearing.

NOT AS IT SEEMS

"Gaylen is working hard to pick up our trail, an' he's using the stops along these roads to gain intelligence. Give me yer dagger," Aine said.

"What for?" I asked, distracted. The air before me seemed to waver and the forest dimmed. "We have to change our looks. I'm going to cut my hair."

For some reason this thought bothered me. "D'ye really think it's necessary?"

She didn't pause, just began to saw at the hair hanging below her chin. "Aye. Ye've got to change yers as well."

I ran my fingers through the riot. It had grown out while I was away with the Templar, but my mam had chopped it again when I returned. It was stiff and smelled of sweat. "Not like to get much shorter," I said.

"No. The color. We've got to change the shade. Ye stick out like a new penny."

"Here now! Ye've no need to offend." I'd hated my bright carrot hair for most of my life, but suddenly at the thought of changing it I wasn't so sure.

"I like yer hair color," Aine said plainly, looking up from her business.

A laugh burst from me. "How could ye? It's horrid."

"No. It's quite lovely, especially when ye're in the sun." I felt my cheeks heat and the freckles begin to flame. Aine didn't pay me any heed.

"How would I change it, anyway? Ye seem to have an idea," I said, intrigued in spite of myself.

"We dye it, as they do the linens."

"Aye?" I said, amazed at the thought.

"We can use the leaves o' the sumac. They're plentiful here."

She continued to hack at her hair, and I watched the auburn curls drop to the ground beside her. Absently I reached for a piece she had cut.

The Holy Vessel's shape hung and glowed in my mind's eye, and my need to hold it, feel it safe in my hands, came on strongly. Aine was fast at my side, her hands cupping my ears and temples as her song flowed. I felt her peace steal into my mind, her whisper that she had me, that everything was well.

My mind drifted. There was a bright light and hands reaching, holding the carving.

Everything in me lurched. "No!" Aine's hum took over the whole of me. *Reach, Tormod. Bring me there.* It was a whisper, a breath of invitation, and without really knowing how I drew her into the vision.

Instantly my scope grew wider, sharper. Sound was clear.

"This piece is nothing to me alone. I need the bowl and the boy. According to the prophecy the power can only be wielded by its Chosen and that one will have all the gifts that Heaven can bestow."

I gasped as the images faded. "That's why they hunt me," I whispered. "I am the Chosen, but no matter what I do, the King will take hold of the carving."

"Ye must be calm, Tormod. Ye will be no good to anyone if ye don't take time to rest. He will no' get it if we don't allow him to," she said.

Ye are calm. We can't rush off tonight, she said, and a soothing wash of power flowed over me. "We need to rest."

My mind was suddenly not as clear as it had been a moment before. I needed to rest. It would wait. What would wait? What had I been thinking or saying? I stared at Aine and felt oddly blank and at peace.

Aine's breathing was harsh and the color was washed from her face. She closed her eyes, waves of exhaustion flowing from her.

"Finish my hair? I can't reach the back," she said. She handed me the dagger. As I took it I saw the tremor that shook her hand.

My own hands felt as if they were not mine to command. I did my best not to yank the soft, fine strands.

"Make it short, like yers," she said. "I feel like I could sleep right here, even with ye tugging."

"Sorry." I lightened up on the pressure of the knife. "Don't ye think this short is a bit much?"

"They're looking for a lad an' lass. I'm going to change into breeks. They'll no' be searching for two lads." She smiled and her face curved softly.

"It will never work," I said. Her eyes and nose were too fine to be a lad. "Ye don't look a bit manly. An' yer voice will surely give ye away."

"We've got to try," she said. "We are easy targets as we are."

My dagger was sharp, but not made for cutting hair. To her credit she made no fuss, though it must have hurt. In the end she looked very different to me. The shape of her face was longer and her eyes, bigger than I remembered.

She went to my pack then and fished out the spare breeks I'd brought and slipped them on. She stepped out of the skirts, adjusted her belt, and pulled the top of the breeks over it. They were too big for her, but they would work.

"Now ye," she said, though I could see her reeling with weariness. "There's sumac just back along the burn. Have more water while I get it. Ye look fit to drop."

I picked up the skin and took a deep gulp. The ground was hard and sharp twigs poked my legs, but the feel was small compared to the tight knot in my stomach that wouldn't go away. I closed my eyes with a sigh, and then all too soon Aine was back, prodding me awake. I struggled to open my eyes. "Leaves?" I asked.

"Aye. We need to soak them to extract the dye." She began to pile sticks and make a fire.

Conversation seemed almost too much. Why was I so tired? Why couldn't I think?

Aine heated some water in the tin from the pack.

"What are ye doin'?"

"Hot water will loosen the color," she said.

I drifted while she worked and came to as she mounded a heap of leaves into the water. A short time later I surfaced as she was mashing them down with a stick, making a fine dark paste. "Ye need to soak yer head."

I looked around blearily. The burn was not far away, but it took a great deal of energy to rise and move toward it. I stripped off my tunic and lay down at its edge. The sound of the running water was melodic. I wanted nothing more than to lie there and sleep for a thousand years.

"Tormod." Aine's soft call roused me and I crawled forward. The water was like ice. It made my head ache, and when I flipped back my hair, it ran down my face and over my back.

A glint of light burst at the corner of my sight, and the face of the Templar lit the space before me. I gasped, my heart pounding wildly. The image had been as clear as if he stood in front of me. I scrambled up the bank to Aine and blurted, "I saw him."

She looked around, leaping to her feet. "Who? Where?"

"The Templar Alexander," I said. "Aine, it was so real I could scarce believe my eyes."

She whuffed out a breath. "He's not here, Tormod," she said. "'Twas just a dream. Ye scared me near to death." She continued to mash the leaves. "Come here. We have to get this on before it dries."

I sat before her, troubled. She began smoothing the thick, cold paste over my head. "He's dead," I said as much to myself as to Aine.

"Aye. I've seen my da in dreams that were so close I never wanted to let them go," she said, rubbing my hair with her fingertips.

"It didn't feel like a dream, or a vision, even. It seemed like he was here, an' real." I felt sheepish about saying more.

"Ye're exhausted. Ye were dreaming." She didn't pause in her work but a flicker of uncertainty washed over her and then me. It was followed by a wave of power. My mind was muddled.

"There. I hope this works," she said.

I stared at her hard, trying to keep my eyes open and remember what we had been talking about. "Ye must let it set while ye sleep. We'll wash it out come morning."

"Ye're joking. All night I'm to sleep in this?" I reached up to feel the odd mess, and she slapped my fingers aside. "Don't touch, an' don't whine. Ye're so tired ye won't even feel it." She was right, my eyes were drooping and I badly needed to lie down.

"D'ye need anything more to eat?" she asked. Cornelius's supplies were saving our lives.

"I'm still hungry, but I'm more tired." My eyes were grainy and I struggled to keep them open. "Are ye going to sleep now?"

"I will in a bit. Ye go on." She was frightened about something. I could feel the tension wafting off her. I pushed myself upright though it was with a cost.

"What's wrong?" I asked.

She paused, her eyes flickering to mine and then away. "It didn't seem real before, but now, I know. There are people coming after us." Between travel and the use of the power, she was exhausted. I felt her tears ready to spring.

"If it's not too sore a burden, I could use yer calming," I said, patting the ground beside me. I sniffed my armpits and wrinkled my nose. "I stink a bit, though, so I won't blame ye if ye don't want to." She laughed weakly. "Honestly though, the powers are rising an' falling so quickly I feel awful."

A flare of nervousness slid through her. "Oh, aye. Whatever ye need," she said.

Her relief was strong in my mind and I fought not to smile. She lay down on her side before me and I wrapped around her. "I can't tell ye that all will be well, Aine, for what I see of the future is a struggle. But ye do have a future. I've seen it. Sleep tonight if that gives ye any peace."

In the end it must have, for she slept soundly until morning. I did not. Unease tormented me.

BETRAYAL WITHIN

Sun slanted through the boughs of the elm above. It lit the back of my eyes with circles of gold and black. I stirred and ran my hands over my head, grimacing when I encountered the stuck and matted stiffness of my hair. My arm was numb where Aine had pillowed her head, and when I moved it, I nearly shoved her off as it tingled back to life.

"What?" she mumbled, snuggling closer while I shifted uncomfortably away.

"My arm's gone dead." I clenched my teeth as hot jolts played beneath my skin. "It's morning. We should be off. I have to wash this out o' my hair an' I'm hungry."

"Aye," she said amicably enough and rolled away. "Lord, I slept like the dead last night," she said, yawning widely. She stood and stretched. It was odd to see her with shorn hair and in breeks instead of a dress. No one in their right mind would see her as a lad, I thought. The breeks looked near indecent, and I felt the color rising to my cheeks. The memory of our kisses and the feel of her curled against me was suddenly much closer than before.

"I'd best see if this comes out," I mumbled.

She didn't bother responding but set to the pack, looking to break our fast as I made my way to the water's edge. "I found some willow bark when I was looking for the sumac. A bit o' tea sounds like heaven just now." She took the water skin, crumbled the bark, and fed it inside, then set to poking the fire back to life.

It was not nearly as easy to wash my head as to just

wet it, I found. The paste stuck and seemed impervious to the water. I scooped up a handful of silt from between the rocks and rubbed it in. By the time I'd gotten it clean, the rest of me was soaked in some way or another so I stripped off my sark and did a quick cold wash. I sloshed back to Aine with water seeping from one of my boots.

"Och!" Aine's eyes traveled over me from head to foot. Red sprouted and crept over her face and feelings of confusion flit through her and then me.

"Did it work?" I could not see my own hair, as it was short, but the pieces that dripped over my eyes looked darker than before.

"Aye. It did. Ye look different," she said shyly. "I like your red better, but this looks fine as well. It's brown."

I tilted my gaze this way and that but could get no real feel for what I looked like. It mattered not, so I gave off trying and pulled my sark back on.

Aine stooped by the fire and put the skin of willow bark tea into the heat. Then she sat back, slowly eating a bannock. My body was thinner, weaker from my trouble with the power. Aine's was as well. In the dappled light of morning, I saw the edges of her. The bones of her arms and legs stuck out from the borrowed clothing that hung on her. The bright orb of the sun glinted through the trees and caught the orange glow of the fire.

I looked up to the sky and without warning everything went black.

"*Where is it?*" The man's voice was unforgiving.

The groan in response made every hair on my head stand.

"*D'ye think we toy with ye, boy?*"

The sound of flesh meeting flesh and the cry of pain that followed curled my insides. My body recoiled from the blow as if I were there, taking it instead.

"No," I murmured. "Please."

I could feel Aine beside me. Her panic was overwhelming, but it was nothing compared to the blossom of agony rippling through me. Again the heavy blow landed, and it felt as if my head would burst. Stars danced before my eyes. I reached for the link, the bridge between Aine and me, but felt only the void.

I clawed my way through the thick veil and she slowly came into focus. "Where am I?" My voice did not feel as if it were my own.

"Tor!" Her cry was hoarse and the spike of joy that whipped through her rocked my sensitive mind. I rolled over and heaved into the leaves. "Here." The water skin was shoved into my hands with force. I took it, but barely had the strength to move.

"I swear ye stopped breathing. I canno' take much more o' this." She was all but babbling and her high-strung emotions battered me, threatening my sanity yet again.

"Shh. Hold my hands an' help me," I said. I didn't remember falling, but I was lying on the hard earth. Aine lifted the skin to my lips and as it washed down my throat I fought to swallow. I was aware of the rocks that dug into my legs and backside, and of the stickiness and sour smell of vomit nearby. Something was horribly wrong. I knew it in the depths of my gut, but no clarity of what ailed me would come to me.

My head was pounding with a ferocious beat that made breathing nearly impossible. The ground was cool beneath me, and yet my body burned as if I were roasting alive. The peace of the forest did nothing but taunt me with the knowledge that I was missing something vital.

"Torquil," I murmured, and then realized that Aine was holding me and humming. I felt her there. My mouth was dry and my lips cracked. I licked and tasted the salty wetness of tears.

"Tormod, are ye truly awake?"

"Torquil is in trouble," I whispered.

"I know. I was there as well." The horror of what we had witnessed pulsed between us.

"How long was I out?" My body felt as if a cairn of rocks was piled atop me. Breathing was difficult, moving worse.

"Moments."

To me it felt like a full day's time. Aine wrapped her arms around me and squeezed tight. Her song was strong in my mind. *Ye will calm. Yer brother is not in danger.* The feel of her body mixed with the suggestion she was feeding me began to numb the worry, but then, something itched the back of my mind. Wrong.

"No!" I murmured, and pulled away as if she were someone I didn't know. "Ye are whispering me? Aine! What are ye doin'?" I couldn't believe it. I had taught and she had learned well. I felt her reach for me again and I shoved her away, furious. She had no right to use the power on me that way. I needed to know what was going on, to use my full faculties to piece together the visions.

"Ye canno' keep overloading yerself. I'm only trying to help, to give you the peace to make it home. Yer body canno' take it," she cried.

I glared at her and she edged away from me. "Ye needed help," she said softly. She shakily crawled to her feet. She was overextended. How long had she been doing this? Tricking me. Taking things from me.

"What else have you stripped from my mind?" I demanded. Aine cowered away from my unchecked anger. "Tell me! Now!" I moved toward her and she backed away. Utter terror lashed out at me, red hot in my tortured mind. It whipped through me, and in response my temper grew. And when it did, Aine's panic expanded yet again.

In a daze of flooded emotion, I watched her turn and run from me. As the forest wind whipped and shrieked, I bolted after her, overtaken by rage. The only thing I could focus on was catching her and making her pay for what she had done.

My breath came in bursts as I pushed my legs to cover the distance between us. She was exhausted, but fear had given her wings. Agile in the breeks, she popped over downed logs and beneath low bushes like a hare in retreat, terrified and determined to get away from me. I read the memories of her uncle as she ran. I saw the broken bones, the swollen lip.

I would never do that, I thought, though I was starting to doubt myself. *Could I be like him? Was I a monster?* Caught up in the turmoil, it was a complete surprise when the edge of land dropped off and Aine disappeared with it.

FRAIL AND FLAWED

"Aine!" I shouted, nearly following her over. My feet slipped as I peered into the ravine below. She was a small bit of white amid a tumble of rock and leaves. "Can ye hear me?" I shouted, frantic.

She made no sound and my fear peaked. *I had done it. I was like him.* This was the vision I had seen. I knew what I would find at the bottom of the gully, and the thought tore my heart in two.

"Hold on! I'm coming!" I shouted. I couldn't feel her, and that frightened me more than anything.

The ravine was sharp and steep. I leapt and slid down in a scramble. Aine lay partially buried in a thick mat of leaves. Earth had showered down on her, and I could only see her face and one foot.

"Aine, can ye hear me?" There was no response and my heart beat with a painful twist. Frantic, I cleared away the muck, uncovering her body bit by bit. She was pale and still, as Aine almost never was.

"Please. Talk to me! Tell me ye're all right! I'm sorry." I brushed the leaves from her hair, lifted her head, and realized that something warm covered my fingers.

My heart stilled. Her blood was bright in the dimness. "Help me, Lord. Please." I tore off the edge of my sark and pressed it to the back of her head.

"Listen to me! Ye will no' die!" I shouted, nearly shaking her. "I have seen it. D'ye hear me?" She had to hear, to understand, but she made no response.

I needed to get inside, to heal her as I had the old Father. Letting my gaze go wide, I called the power to me with barely leashed fury. "Come! Now!"

And it did, Lord help me, it came. Fueled by my desperation, the power leapt at my command — fast, strong, and very much beyond my control. The rush struck me numb. I could not move, nor pull my hands from her head. We were sealed to each other as heat poured through our joined bodies, searing a path I could not stop or contain.

It was like the bairn. The realization stoked my furor. Like a wild thing, it rose and grew. Without Aine to tamp it down the power rushed and my shields completely collapsed. Raw energy surged. Light. Dark. Heat. Cold. The world convulsed around me and utter agony was my only sensation.

BEYOND THE PALE

"*Awaken.*" The voice came to me as if from afar. It was firm and demanding, yet I could not rouse the energy to care. I stayed in the dark, clinging to the cold. I'd done it again. My life was forfeit. My pain for Aine was all-consuming. I'd lost them: the Templar, Seamus, the bairn, and now Aine. I didn't deserve to go on. I didn't want to.

"*Aine lives. Call on the Lord. Do it now.*" I was adrift, alone, dying, and talking to the dead. "*Ye have been chosen. Ye agreed. Do what ye were called to do. She will live. Wake now and move quickly.*"

The dream of the Templar was so real I could do naught but return to the waking world. "Our Father, who art in heaven . . ." The prayer of Our Lord whispered in the depths of my mind. Light pressed my eyelids with a violence that made my guts heave. My head felt dislodged from my body. There was something beneath me, at the same time hard and soft.

Aine. I rolled to my side, putting an ear to her chest and listening to her breath. Light, fast. Not the way it should be, but still, she lived.

I needed to get help. "Hold on, Aine." I stared at her, sick at heart, then scanned the area wildly. I knew I hadn't the strength to carry her, nor could I use the power to heal her. I had to find help. Though it killed me to leave her there, I bolted back to camp and thundered out of the clearing. *She canno' die. No' like this. No' at my hands.*

The memory of her still, white face made me mad with fear. I rode as if haunted toward a village we had bypassed earlier, opening myself to it. The roar of thoughts and feelings drew me like stone, but also left me near faint in the saddle. *I will no' fail.* I set myself to the commands of shielding with a will that burst a sheen of sweat over the whole of my body.

The village sat at the base of a vale deep in the woods. When I came upon the inn, it was as if I were riding into the jaws of hell. Frightened but determined, I dropped from the horse at a run, but before I had gone two paces I knew that this place was probably a huge mistake. *They* were here.

I pulled my cloak close about me and softly began the whisper. Then I stepped into the shadows of the inn.

FAMILIAR FACES

They sat in disarray all around the inn, lounging, drinking, and laughing. The soldiers. Pockface included. I willed myself to move slowly. *Just a lad from the village. Nothing more.* Sweat beaded along my brow as the draw on the power slowly ate away at my shielding.

"Ale for ye?" A serving lass came with a tankard.

"Aye." I kept my voice low and soft. No one marked my entrance, but my heart still hammered wildly. I kept my head low and watched the other patrons through downcast eyes.

The leader sat across from me, oblivious to my presence. A parchment was spread on the table before him.

I had to get help, but who and how could I ask without drawing attention to myself? The server passed through a long, dark curtain into another room of the inn. I followed her with my eyes, and when she did not return, I stood, willing my shaking legs to move. I crept over to the wall and changed benches, as if I needed the warmth of the fire. If I could get into the kitchen unnoticed, perhaps the inn's owner would be able to help.

The leader's back was now to me, the edge of the parchment clear from where I sat. In the upper corner was a signet marked in wax. My stomach flipped and light burst suddenly before me. A golden ring dangled from a chain. A dark room lit by a multitude of candles. A warm breeze where no wind should have been. *Send the boy to Philippe. Bring the Holy Vessel to me.*

I came to myself knowing two things — that I had heard the voice in a vision before and that my whisper had faltered. I dropped my head and hunched my shoulders, wondering how many sets of eyes were staring in my direction.

Tormod? The voice touched my mind softly, and I snapped my head up in disbelief. Across the room a man was bound and huddled on the floor.

Bertrand? To frame the question sorely taxed my overwrought senses.

He recognized me even with hair of deep brown. I knew it was ridiculous trying to disguise myself this way. His warning rang out strongly. *Get out o' here. These men are killers and they are hunting ye.*

Though my head was throbbing and my arms and legs shivered with the backlash of power use, I mind-spoke to Bertrand. *I need yer help.* I sent a mental image of what had happened to Aine and without pause pulled the power and began the whisper again. This time I stirred the soldiers' anger and inflamed their exhaustion.

All around the room men began to bristle. A big meaty hand gripped the mug the serving woman put on his table. Another closed over the first and yanked. Ale splashed in a wave, dousing two others who sat behind them. Benches flew back and tables were shoved aside. Men's voices rose in heat and the brawl began.

I sent the whisper wider, fanning the flame of annoyance. Sweat soaked my hair and back. The room seemed to waver and pulse before me as I stumbled, nearly blind, to Bertrand's side and crouched to free him. We were overlooked and without interference slipped out the rear door.

Even the light of day was too much to bear. I fumbled my way to the horse and dragged my body into the saddle. Bertrand was close behind, mounted on a horse he'd taken.

"Hurry, lad. It won't be long before they notice I'm gone." He took in my ragged appearance at a glance. "Ye're in sore shape. Can ye ride?" he asked, his concern flaring within my mind. I nodded, barely seeing him as the forest wavered around me.

The horses took off like twin arrows as the furor of the men inside surged behind me. They had noticed Bertrand's escape, and they were coming.

The horse's muscles bunched beneath me. The wind tore at my clothes and hair, and my surroundings slid into a blur of shadow. We had to get away, to reach Aine.

222

Without warning a strong flow of power radiated around and within me, and a new strength became mine. *Trees.* The thought and direction were strong.

Quickly I loosed the earth around the base of a great, long-dead trunk and flinched as it thundered down onto the road just behind Bertrand. I felt another and reached. It fell. And then one more. The road was littered, impassible.

Only the thought of Aine kept me conscious, and when I reached for the reassurance of her essence, I found her vital connection was gone. I nearly gave in then to the encroaching dark.

Hold on, Tormod. A whisper flit through me and again the waft of strength came to me. Whose words, and whose strength was it? The wind whipped and my thoughts were torn away.

"Are we nearly there?" Bertrand shouted from behind.

"Aye! Beyond the bend. Beware the drop." I reached it in moments and leapt from my mount. With cold dread I scrambled down the incline and dug at the piles of leaves, confused.

Then, all at once, my heart froze. My mind refused to believe. Aine was not there.

GONE MISSING

"Are ye sure this is the place ye left her?" Bertrand asked. We combed the area. I knew it was right. Aine was just unaccountably not here.

"The leaves have been flattened." I pointed. "She lay there." Bertrand was looking about carefully. I was pacing and frantic.

"Mayhap she was no' as bad off as ye thought. She might have awakened after ye left."

I looked at him sharply. "An' what?" I demanded, my temper rising before I could control it. "Climbed back up that incline and hied herself to break her fast?" It was surely impossible. I stooped where I had left her, staring hard at the leaves.

"Aye. I suppose ye're right. If she were wounded as ye said, there would be some trace o' her passage." He rubbed his head and looked around the area.

"I have an idea," I said abruptly.

"What's that?" asked Bertrand.

I paid him no heed, but set immediately to it. The power came swiftly at my reach and I began to read the forest, thinking of Aine, using the power as I had seen her do. It did not come to me as clearly as it did for Aine. But then, wraithlike forms suddenly filled my head and a vision crashed down with bone-jarring strength. Men in the forest, moving with stealth. One leaning over Aine's body. I strained to see, to feel. And in that moment I understood. I felt nothing from him at all. Gaylen.

I snapped to with a lurch and my stomach heaved. Pain slammed my temples and I dropped to my knees, holding my head. Waves of agony rolled through my body. Black seeped in before my eyes.

"Tormod!" I heard Bertrand, but I could not speak or move. The power ripped through me and everything felt afire. The second vision that descended and filled my mind's eye was one I had forgotten. One Aine had dulled into something that I barely recognized.

The lash hissed. I heard it catch and cut. The scream that tore through the silence brought a pain to my heart so deep and resounding that tears flowed from my eyes. *Torquil.*

"Tormod, ye must stop!" Bertrand was shaking me.

"What am I to do?" I stared at him, unseeing. "Bertrand, what can I do?" It was more than I could bear. I wanted to close my mind's eye and die.

Stop! Now! The command came at me with the power of a blow. I felt broken, my head and body shattered. Voices came at me in a jumble. The Templar's,

225

Bertrand's, and Aine's, all seemed to echo within me. Thoughts collided and crashed. Thunder roared in my ears. Breath rattled in my chest.

Focus. The word came at me insistently.

Ground. The solid strength of the land was thrust deep into my head and I latched on for life.

And I gave in, reaching. "Shield." My voice was harsh and strained.

Bertrand knelt by my side, his hands strong on my head. All around me the swirl of the land's powers flowed. I was safe, for now. I lay as still as the dead.

"Tormod, ye've barely any internal shielding! I can't imagine how ye've survived this long. I know of no one who could withstand direct contact with the power, unprotected. Be still now while I probe," he admonished, mumbling to himself as he went along. I felt him inside my head. Moving, weighing, healing. "Your powers are much askew. Something has burned out the bit o' yer mind that protects the gifted from the use o' the power." His words were like the chatter of woodland animals. I heard him but had not the time to spare for listening. I was weak and tired, consumed with the choice I knew I must make.

"The power drains any who attempt to use it, but this is far more. It's worse than ere I've seen, and the damage is progressing."

His expression was grave. "Yer inner protections have been stripped from ye, lad. Usually with rest, the body can rejuvenate on its own after exposure, but yers is no'. An' despite each shield I build, an' no matter how much I encourage healing, they won't take. They're unraveling as fast as I can weave them."

His words held a panic that was bringing me lower by the moment. I thought he would have answers, but these were not the responses I wanted to hear.

"There's a tendril of power tied to ye from some-where else. I don't know what 'tis. I dare no' sever it for it stretches too far away for me to see the origin. Ye need more healing than I can provide. We have to get ye back to the preceptory, to the high healers."

My head was pounding. "No. Aine needs me. I have to rescue her from the Bruce's men. An' yet, my brother needs me. The men o' Philippe will take and hurt him badly. The family boat will be set afire. The Abbot will be kidnapped. So many things. Too many crises." My head was pounding and I felt my blood rush with fever.

"Ye must still yerself, Tormod. Tell me all that's happened."

Whatever he was doing gave me enough peace and strength to answer him. Briefly and quickly I told him all that had happened, from my running from home and meeting Aine to the slow ruin of my powers and Aine's

terrible accident. I left out the bairn, as I could not, even now, bear to think about what I'd done.

"Aine is injured and taken, and my family, the carving, and the Abbot are all in grave danger. What am I supposed to do?" Helplessness was clawing great rents in my soul.

"I will go to the Bruce and care for Aine. I am a healer. I've set a temporary shield in place that should hold until ye make it to the preceptory. Ye will go there. Now, with all haste." He moved to his horse and climbed into the saddle. "The soldiers will be looking for our path. We can confuse them by splitting up."

It was the right thing to do, but how could I leave Aine? He sensed my hesitation. "Go, lad. I'll get her an' we'll find ye. I promise!"

AN UNWELCOME CHOICE

The dread of not knowing what was to come was like a sour berry in my mouth. And as if I were a plaid unraveling, Bertrand's healing was failing with every league I traveled.

"Work yer shields." Bertrand's parting advice prodded

me as I traveled. The road grew dark and the moon hung as a bare sliver in the sky that waned as I crossed the wooded land toward the coast. The keening wind played deep in my ears as thoughts of losing Aine battled with those of losing everything else. My eyes were gritty and the ache of backlash pulsed in my jaw. I worked my shields as I rode, trying to break free of the thoughts that haunted me.

Focus. The sound of night crowded my ears. *Ground.* I reached for the solid earth beneath the hooves of my mount.

And with no warning at all a searing pain slammed into my shoulder, knocking me from the horse.

I hit the ground with bone-jarring contact and hissed as my fingers groped and caught the shaft of the arrow that had pierced me. Out of habit and desperation, I reached for the power.

No, Tormod! The voice that filled my mind demanded that I take heed, but it was beyond too late. Power came at my frantic call, crashing its way through me. Dark became light and flowed once more to dark. Heat flowed in my veins and my body felt as if I had burst into flame. The pain in my shoulder was nothing compared to the agony tearing apart my mind and body.

I hadn't felt the attack coming. I couldn't sense it.

That should have explained it all.

A REUNION OF SORTS

"Nice o' ye to rejoin the waking world, Tormod." My guts surged to my throat as Gaylen gripped my hair and yanked until my neck was stretched and I opened my eyes. I felt the blade press against the sensitive skin there. "Where is it?" he said in a dead soft voice that made me quiver. "Don't think to play with me, Tormod. I guarantee it will go badly for yer precious lass."

Aine. "What are ye talkin' about?" I stalled.

I had hoped that he was bluffing, but his next words squashed the notion. "The thing that ye found, Tormod. The vessel o' power that the whole o' the world is now seeking. Ye will give it to me," he said in a way that brooked no argument. "There are things no man can withstand."

I stared hard, trying to understand how he could know about the Holy Vessel and why it meant anything to him. "Ye shot me? Why?"

He looked at me as if I were daft. "Ye were fleeing," he said. "I need ye." He said it as if it were the most natural thing in the world. My pain and injury were nothing that troubled his conscience.

"Why would ye need me? I'm nothing." I struggled to find a way out of this.

"Oh, no, ye're worth quite a bit to many, as is the thing that ye found." His eyes were eerie in the dark. Blank like his soul's signature.

"I don't have it," I said boldly.

"Aye, but ye will take me to it," he replied a bit too smugly.

"What makes ye think I would do that?" Bravado in the face of the knife at my throat, but I felt good for it still.

He was unmoved. "If ye don't, yer fair lass will pay the fee."

"I'll kill ye if ye lay one hand on her!" I snarled.

"Touching. Young love," he mocked. "Shame I'll have to cut it short this way." He pressed the knife harder and I felt it pierce my skin. Not by much, but enough to sting.

"Get up." He took the knife from my throat and yanked me to my feet. "There are some willing to pay just about anything to possess this thing an' ye. I am no' such a one, but I would no' turn from an opportunity thrust my way." With no preamble he reached down and snapped off the arrow about a thumb's width from the wound. Pain ripped through me and I nearly dropped in a faint.

"Here now. I thought as a trainee to be God's hero,

ye'd be a bit hardier than that," he said with a smirk. I wondered what it was about Templars that set him off. I'd never heard anyone utter even the slightest degree of disrespect toward the Order.

I could scarcely catch my breath before he shoved me forward. "On yer horse," he snapped. I stumbled and landed hard against my mount. The arrowhead twisted and I cried out.

He showed no pity, just remounted and waited with thinly veiled contempt while I struggled to drag myself into the saddle.

We rode through the night, hard and fast. And as the pearl pink of the morning sky dawned, we continued. I ate astride from the remnants of Cornelius's sack and drank until the skin was dry. When I could hold my water no longer, I begged leave to stop. Gaylen allowed it but watched me carefully and kept his hand on the lead of my horse. Throughout the whole of the trip I worked my shields, praying for the moment I could attempt escape.

For his part, Gaylen spoke only when necessary. He had the constitution of a hardened soldier. I believed he would ride for days on end with little discomfort, but it was not that way for me. My last call on the power was the worst I had ever attempted. I felt as if I were dead inside. I could feel nothing beyond the endless pain in my shoulder and the grief in my heart. *The world would be better served if I let Gaylen kill me here and now,* I thought, *rather than to give him the Holy Vessel.*

As low as I felt, I might have goaded him into killing me had the image of Aine not hung all the while before my mind's eye. *Please, Lord, help her.* The phrase became a prayer I repeated hundreds of times as I rode. I had to live, to make sure she was safe. To make sure they all were safe. In this I had no choice.

"Move along. I only have to keep ye in one piece to get the artifact. There are many degrees to the state o' being alive," he said coldly.

I looked to him sharply. Could he read my thoughts? Was that how he knew?

He glared at me and I realized that I was just standing there, wavering. I wanted to move but couldn't.

"It will no' come cheaply, this thing you ask, de Nogaret. When the time comes, we will expect to be repaid."

"You have my word."

"It's no' yer word that I'm needing."

"Yes. You have his as well."

"Say it."

"Don't test me, Gaylen. The King will give you his support. Troops and men against the English."

The hillside came once more into view. "Move, I said!" Gaylen snapped.

Nausea bubbled in my throat. Every movement I made jarred the shaft of the arrow and fresh fiery jags of pain assaulted me. Blood seeped through my tunic and plaid. It was cold, wet, and sticky, and my shoulder pulsed. I remounted and we set off once again.

Heavy rain began to fall late into the night of the second day. Time passed in a haze of exhaustion. Only the stride of the horse echoed in my ears for company, and I barely clung to consciousness. Four wet days in, my body rejected any shielding I could call to place. Five days in, we came to the shore where a boat awaited our arrival, as did several olive-skinned swarthy men. No questions were asked, nor fares paid. We boarded and were underway in a time barely marked by the candle.

I huddled in a corner where Gaylen had shoved me, out of the wind and away from his ever-present gaze. I welcomed the darkness that crept closer as blood ebbed from my wound.

I tried to pull the shaft free only once; the pain was too heady for me to bear. The arrowhead was lodged deep in muscle and tissue. And though I called on the power to try and heal myself, nothing came. All was silent and dead to me.

I was stripped of my gifts and alone, abandoned. I willed sleep to take me away or death to claim me, but neither happened. Instead the image of the Lady came to me, the woman whose likeness had been carved, whose essence still clung to the aged piece of wood when last I had seen it. She was just as I remembered. Her eyes of amber were filled with sadness.

And then without warning, before my mind's eye, I suddenly saw Aine. She lay on her side, her head wrapped in bloody linen. Her eyes were glazed and she drifted in the other sight. Then, all at once, it was as if we were looking directly at each other.

I sat up quickly, jostling the arrow shaft, and the pain yanked me from the connection. "No," I murmured, and Gaylen drew near. I lay back down and feigned sleep, trying desperately to reestablish the link, but it was to no avail. She was gone, and yet, not lost. Aine was alive and trying to contact me. Nothing had ever been as welcome.

UNHOLY HEAT

Two days passed as we made our way back to the shores of Edinburgh, but for the most part, I did not much mark the time. My body was wracked with a heat that drew me in and out of a place that could only be the Hell straight out of the priest's Sunday sermons.

Flames licked my legs, blistering the skin and roasting my bones. I was immobile, though I wanted to thrash and scream with agony. Conversations happened around me, but I couldn't open my eyes or make a sound.

"He's not going to make it, and I will not pull into shore with a dead boy on my ship."

"It's just a fever. Nothing more."

"Fever is deadly. It can take a village in a week."

"No' this fever. 'Tis just the wound. He's no' yer responsibility once we land."

Faces drifted in and out of my sight. Torquil. The Abbot. The Templar. Aine. Bertrand. The bairn. Cornelius. Visions. Dreams. Nightmares. I could make no sense of them. I saw a palace surrounded by sand and a crypt deep beneath the earth. I recognized a prison cell, the smell of blood, and the taste of fear.

"Stand, or I will drag you up by the shaft o' that arrow." Gaylen's voice held a threat that was real, and I struggled to wake and crawl to my knees. "We are here and the horses have been taken to shore. It's time."

I could not climb down the ladder and so was lowered by a rope around my chest. The pain in my shoulder made me insensible. I could barely breathe when they dropped me into the coracle and we were taken ashore.

Once there, it took the last of my strength to remount and I lay along the horse's neck. "Where are ye takin' me?" I murmured.

"To the preceptory, lad. Where else would a Templar's apprentice seek healing?"

My shocked look made him laugh. "Did ye think I did no' know the Holy Vessel is within those walls? Closed to the world, but not to one of their own in need."

"But I'm not an apprentice," I protested.

"You are something to them, an' that's no lie. They are going to great lengths to try and find ye. I will just aid them in the search."

Conversation with Gaylen was confusing. Mayhap it was the pain. Looking for me? If the Templars were seeking me, it was not because they wanted me safe. I remembered the vision. They were angry that I had used the Vessel. I had given away the secret to those who would use it for gain.

It did not matter what I thought, however. Gaylen had a plan, and getting me inside the preceptory was a part of it. I thought of the Abbot and prayed that I was not too late. If I were in time and could get him alone and tell him what was happening, they could arrest Gaylen and stop whatever was his intention.

I needed a plan, but in the late hours of night, when finally we gained the twisting path I remembered well, I still had not come to anything.

I tried, in vain, to summon even the slightest bit of the power of the land. Nothing came but a rising sense of panic. I shivered as the wind cut strongly across the hillside. The gates were as I remembered, enormous and impregnable, but Gaylen approached with no hesitation.

"Who are ye and what d'ye want? It's late," called down the guard.

"An injured boy seeking a healer. He is one of yers," said Gaylen.

"What say ye?"

"We seek the Abbot. Wake him," said Gaylen with an authority I wondered at. The guard did as he was told. Dead to the power, I could detect nothing, but I wondered if Gaylen had the ability to whisper a push. I hunched against the cold, fighting off the waves of blackness that beat at me.

The gate opened slowly, and the sense of awe I felt

the few times I had been here returned. It was late and the grounds were quiet. I saw the shapes of men patrolling the wall walks atop the gate, but all the interior shops and huts were dark.

Two armed guards awaited us. "Come," said a large knight near me. He was imposing, and yet I found reassurance in his presence. Exhaustion made my legs drag. Gaylen's palm was rough on my neck, pulling me up and jarring the shaft. I jammed my teeth together, hissing.

I struggled to stay on my feet and walk between the guards. By the time we reached the great kirk and the top of the winding staircase that led to the Abbot's chambers, I could barely catch a breath.

Gaylen shoved me inside, and I fought waves of dizziness as the dark of the stairs became the light of the study. Seated at the desk across from me was someone as different from the Abbot as I could ever imagine.

"Ye had better have a good reason to call me from prayer at this time o' night." He was tall, wide, and loud, though attired as the Abbot had been in brown robe and tonsured head.

"Where is the Abbot?" I blurted. I was too late. The quick rush of alarm disoriented me, and I squeezed the edge of the desk to keep from fainting. The movement reopened the wound and a fresh spurt of blood soaked my sark. What if I were too late for all of them?

"Who are ye to speak to me in this manner?" the monk asked imperiously.

"Tormod MacLeod," I said. In my mind I whispered, *Templar's apprentice and friend to the Abbot and Grand Master.*

The monk's eyes grew wide and he looked me over from head to foot. "Take him to confinement."

I gasped and Gaylen protested. "He is injured an' needs healing."

The Abbot's replacement was unimpressed. "Ye have delivered yer charge. I see no reason for ye to remain within these walls. Ye will be escorted out lest ye find yerself verily confined."

Gaylen's eyes narrowed, and though I could sense nothing from him, I knew there was a contained fury simmering. This had not been a part of his plans. Though I did not relish the prison cell awaiting, Gaylen could not follow, nor could he find and take the Holy Vessel.

As they escorted me away, I could not hide the smirk that creased my countenance.

"This is far from over." His soft threat met my ears alone. "I wouldn't get too comfortable in yer room."

HER CHOSEN

The cell was a small, bare room on the far east corner of the preceptory. It was dark and the pallet thin, but neither of these were a concern to me. A healer had attended the arrow wound before I'd been brought here, and a light sleeping draft dulled the ache not quite eliminated by the healing. He had been an ordinary healer, not one of the gifted, for he noticed nothing of my other many distresses. I drifted in a half doze, wondering what would become of me.

I had no shields, no strength, no friends, and no hope. I sought the darkness, but the image of the carving filled the space behind my lids with light. I buried my head in my arms and willed it to go away. I hurt inside and out. I was beyond tired and completely alone. I was good to no one. My tears flowed like the rain drizzling down beyond my prison cell.

Sleep came a long time later, but the image of the carving remained bright. At some point in the night, the wood wore away and the woman emerged. The real woman, who had appeared to me only a few times before. Her soft amber eyes glowed with compassion and she stretched out her arms to embrace me. Peace and love were mine for the taking.

I woke with a start, my heart pounding, and the pull that I had been feeling — the odd connection that grew more strained as I had moved farther and farther from home, that had been severed when I lost touch with the power — was mine again and had multiplied tenfold. The power was mine. The duty was mine. I could not ignore the call this time. I felt it clear through the walls. The promise I had made was not something I had kept.

I stood and moved to the door of my cell, and without hesitation I drew the power. To my surprise, it came, harsh and heady, but mine to command nevertheless. Beyond the door I felt the life of my guards. Two hearts beat.

The lad needs to use the privy. Sweating and shivering, I pushed. *Walk him there now.* I heard the mumble of the guard as he approached, and then I targeted the second. *He needs water. Get it.* I clapped my hands to my ears as the pressure of the whisper nearly broke me.

The turn of the key was loud in the silence. Quickly I switched back to the first guard. *Get food from the kitchen.* I was rewarded with the shuffle of booted feet as he moved away and the second followed in thrall.

I stepped from the cell and moved down the hall. Rush torches sat high in brackets, sending thin plumes of light flickering along the flagstones. In the shadows I whispered, *There is no one here.*

Though a number of guards stood sentinel at regular intervals, not a one turned my way or made any move to stop my escape. The use of power was burning inside me. I felt its path hollowing my body with every step, every push I sent. It mattered not. I was hers to command and she was calling me forward.

Tormod . . .

The voice in my head nearly knocked my legs from beneath me. *Aine?* Reaching was worse then trying to push, much more difficult and costly.

Ye have to stop. The power is killing ye!

I have been chosen, Aine. She is calling. It was as if I were talking to myself and yet I heard Aine clearly.

Whisper no more! We will do it for ye. The voice was not Aine's this time, but Bertrand's and the waft of relief I felt hearing him was tremendous. Bertrand had found her. She was safe. And then I felt their flow of power, taking over where I had left off. Their whisper, even from a distance, was as strong as mine.

Slowly, as if in a dream, I made my way through the compound. The rain slashed down on my face, plastering my hair and dripping into my eyes. I passed the shops and huts, then circled around the training grounds and the kirk.

I was not cold, though the wind and rain pelted down. Within me, the tug grew stronger, and it felt as if many small fires lit a path through my body. The grounds of the preceptory were large, but soon the rear gates came into view. To the east an ancient burial grove lay. I knew without a doubt that the Holy Vessel lay somewhere within.

The cairn sat high on the hillside, an ancient crumble of stone that was gray and ravaged. Vines had twined over the entrance, but the sliver of space behind the great slab beckoned me. I moved toward it with an anticipation that churned like hunger. The space was tight, but not for someone of the Abbot's size, nor for someone of mine.

I stepped in, and my breath grew shallow as the whole of the cairn appeared to close in around me. And the cold wetness seemed to sink beyond my skin. Seeing human bones stacked in the open, I felt I might be buried here, in the dark, forever.

A GIFT

Ye're o' the light. Push it away. The voice echoed in the depths of my mind. I remembered the Templar speaking those very words to me long ago, but why now should I hear them?

Hail Mary, full o' grace ... The prayer sounded softly in my head and I brought it to my lips. "The Lord is with thee . . ." All at once heat poured through me and before my eyes a host of sparkling lights illuminated a trail.

With new peace I moved through the space.

I would not have thought the hills beneath the preceptory to be riddled with burial chambers, but there were many. Cavern after cavern, the once cleanly wrapped bodies were naught but dust and bones. It didn't seem a place the Holy Vessel should reside, but I knew it was here. The trail of light and thrum of life in a place bereft of both was strong. It grew as I walked, racing through my veins, filling me with determination. I passed through many rooms connected by tunnels of earth, while the past lives of all of the men who lay there flit gently through me. It was like my first experience with the sacred bowl and pedestal. I knew those laid to rest here walked in the light. These monks were God's Chosen, as was I. I had forgotten that in my struggle.

The pull was strong. It grew as I walked, the walls coming closer as I moved deeper into the cairn and the remains of the dead, less. Rounding a bend I came up short, surprised to see that the space I'd entered had a distinct end. The light continued to sparkle and the pulse of the power called me on, but the rear wall of dirt and tangled root went no farther. I moved closer, holding my breath in anticipation.

On a shelf that looked much like every other in the cairn, it sat, quiet and unassuming. The plain wooden box was banded and sealed with iron studs and lay beside several very old jars. I'd never seen the holder constructed for it, but I knew without a doubt that the Holy Vessel lay inside.

I slid my fingers along the edge of it, trembling as the familiar warmth and welcome only the Holy Vessel could give flowed.

Slowly I lifted the lid. Light flashed in the dark behind my eyes. I dropped to my knees, the open box tight in my grasp. The carving and bowl glowed with unearthly heat while images flooded my weary mind.

"What is your name, boy?"

Men in arms. Blue and gold. Torquil tied at the wrists.

"My name is Tormod."

"No!" I wanted to shout and to wake from this vision, but there was more I was meant to see.

"It's me ye want. I am the red-haired one ye seek."

My roar of denial echoed through the cavern, but even as I surfaced from the vision my mind was sifting through the many instances and conversations Torquil and I had exchanged. Torquil was gifted! And I knew he felt responsible for all that had befallen me. He would use the power to convince them, and he would be taken.

I hugged the box to me, hunched like a wounded animal. Torquil would be imprisoned. He would be beaten, lashed. He would lose himself in the pain. No. No, no, no. It was not going to happen. I would not allow it. I was the Chosen. The prophecy said that I would have all the gifts Heaven and earth could bestow. I would use them well. I would change what was to come and make it the future that I chose it to be.

With determination I reached inside the box.

Heat and energy sizzled and burst as it had the very first time I had united the pieces of the Holy Vessel. Fire coursed through my veins, racing through my body, taking me to a place where I no longer existed. Time froze. Breath ceased. Life, as I knew it, dropped into stillness.

And something within me changed.

THE COVENANT REBORN

The cold dirt of the crypt pressed against my face. I opened my eyes slowly, feeling my aching body shift and creak as I rolled to my back. It took a moment to remember where I was and what I had been doing, but when I did, the rush of panic brought me instantly to my knees. Torquil. I looked around quickly and saw that the Holy Vessel sat apart in the box beside me. Even in my jumbled-up state I longed to wrap my fingers around them once again. The carving glowed a sullen white in the darkness, a soft beacon that lit the place well enough to see. I knew that I must hurry home, but what to do about the Holy Vessel? It had called me. I needed it. There were things I had yet to do. But the idea of taking it from here filled me with dread.

Then a thought came to me: If the pieces were not together, then the whole would not be in jeopardy.

Quickly I placed the bowl reverently in its space, closed the box, and laid it back on the shelf where I'd found it. With pleasure I wrapped my fingers around the carving and moved through the darkened space toward home.

The carving lit my route through the underground tunnels as if I carried a torch and had been here a dozen times before. Through a fissure in the darkness I stepped into the night. The opening was far beyond the gates of the preceptory, long in the direction of home. With the beat of my heart loud in my ears, I climbed the rocks to the top of the rise and faded into the trees. I ran, then, as I hadn't in a very long time, since before any of this had begun. I was my da's runner. I was fast. I would make it.

Off in the distance came the cry of the wolves. They had frightened me sorely when first I'd run through these woods, but they seemed now only a small part of an extremely vast world.

I cut a path where none existed, as the trees around me whispered of power and danger and trouble pressed like the breath of a ghost on my neck. My footfalls pounded in time with the thump of the sporran against my waist and the heat of the carving streaked warmth through my body. Memories of visions haunted my passing, and fear built a lump in my stomach that grew as I ran. *The boat afire. Torquil in agony. Aine, white and bleeding.* I ran as fast as my legs would take me, praying heart and soul that I would reach them in time.

And when at last I came on the great boulder in the village square, the sense that something was wrong had become so strong that my legs trembled beneath me. Though I knew that I shouldn't, I reached for the power, stretching ahead for the feel of my family. What came in the wake of that reach chilled the blood in my veins.

Desperate heartbreak. Mam.

I stumbled to the door of the hut as the carving seemed to burst into flame at my waist.

CONFRONTATION

My mam's frightened, tear-streaked face looked at me as if I were expected. "Tormod!" My name escaped on a sob. "Get away from here! Run!"

"A touching scene," Gaylen said mockingly, as he held the knife he had used on me up to my mam's throat. "Now why would he be leaving such a loving family reunion so soon?" His eyes narrowed. "Carefully put whatever 'tis ye're gripping in that sporran gently on the table."

"Mam, where is the family?" I asked quietly, shifting toward the table, desperately trying to stall for the time to think of a way out of this.

Gaylen pressed the knife a little harder and a soft cry escaped her. "No tricks, little man. There's no one about to save either o' ye. They're off to the laird to set up a search party for yer brother."

My heart nearly stopped.

"But they're no' going to find him, Tormod. He's long away now. Takin' yer place with the soldiers of Philippe."

Mam's terror lashed out at me, and I stumbled against the table with the force of it. I wanted to lunge at him and cut out his lying tongue. Torquil could not be gone. That would mean that I had failed him, had failed them all. Again.

"Aye. Philippe will pay far more for that little trinket ye hold than the Church. They came to me as well."

His words were slippery in my head, battering my shielding. I felt it breaking down moment by moment.

"Put down the artifact, Tormod, or she will never see another day."

I felt the truth in what he said. My body began to shake as I looked into my mam's eyes and could feel nothing but her fear.

Distance yerself! The command startled me into motion. I reached for the steadiness of the earth, and, as the first of the shielding commands enveloped me, I was able to think once more.

"Send her away and I will give ye what ye want. I will come with ye to deliver the package." As I silently worked at the second command, I changed direction and walked toward the fire instead of the table.

I drew the carving from my sporran and held it out toward the flame. "I will burn it before yer eyes if ye don't release her unharmed." I closed my eyes a moment, pressing hard and out, and my shield snapped into place. The power was mine to command, even if it was only for a while.

Ye canno' carry it without me, I whispered toward Gaylen.

I saw the pressure of his knife lessen. He was not immune to my whisper. I took a step closer and held it over the fire. *Let the woman go. She will hinder yer progress.*

And then, suddenly, Aine's hum filled my mind and a flow of power with the essence of Bertrand fleshed out the strength of my whisper.

Almost against his will, Gaylen moved toward the door with my mam still pinned in place before him. I pushed again, sweat beading up on my forehead and beneath my arms, and he opened the door and shoved her outside.

Mam did not hesitate. She bolted away, no doubt racing for help.

Gaylen stood with his back to the door. His breath was harsh and in his eyes burned an anger that hammered my overtaxed senses.

"Ye think to challenge me?" he said.

252

I moved away from the fire, gripping the carving, its warmth nearly burning my fingers. I began gathering strands of loose power to myself.

"I don't know what ye're talking about," I bluffed, working the suggestion into his mind. *Ye need to be away from here. Men are coming.*

He drew himself up straighter, looming over me in the dimness, and fury pounded against my shielding. I pulled my dagger from its sheath and the dance between us began.

I waited for him to make the first move as I had been taught by the Templar. In his anger, he was impatient and leapt forward, slashing deep toward my middle with his knife. I darted out of the way and shoved a stool in his direction, but he tossed it aside with little effort. "Ye've a bit o' training, I see. Well, it's no' nearly enough."

I felt the power grow, then suddenly pool around him. His next slash caught my tunic, but I moved quickly and the cut missed my skin.

"Give it to me," he said, using a compulsion so strong I fought myself to keep from obeying. The carving in my hand was heavy. I felt my shielding begin to thin along with my resolve.

"Hand me the artifact an' ye will live to try an' save yer brother. Continue to play with me an' I will kill ye now, and then I will kill all yer family, starting with yer dear, sweet mam." Images poured through my mind. Tortures he planned to commit. Cruelties he would find pleasure fulfilling.

I reared from the visions, sickened.

"Yes, ye see now what I can do. What I want to do, if ye but give me one reason. But it will end here, if ye are but a good lad an' do exactly what ye're told." I felt his whisper deep in my mind. *Ye are only a lad. This charge is too great.* I was wavering. If I did as he said, no one would get hurt. Gaylen was moving toward me with the knife in his hand, sweeping it back and forth.

Ground! The voice of the Templar rang in my ears.

"Alexander?" I said aloud, stunned.

"Calling yer friend will d'ye no good," Gaylen taunted. "There are warrants out all over the land. He will not be coming to yer rescue." The knife jabbed toward me and I darted to the side, barely avoiding it.

Ground, Tormod. Do it now!

Suddenly the room began to tilt. *No,* I thought, I could not let this happen. The darkness was closing in on me and I was powerless to stop it. A vision was descending as Gaylen was advancing.

Paper beneath a soldier's hand. A seal in the right-hand corner. Familiar. I had seen it . . . on a ring. I felt Aine's concentration and the vision widened. Words caught from the corner of my eye. Closer. Clearer. *To be taken alive. Templar Alexander Sinclair.*

I felt the first cut of the blade, a knick on my arm. He came at me strong and hard and I stepped aside, stabbing toward his body. The slice cut away a bit of his tunic. Blood glistened on my blade.

"Stop playing with me, lad. Put the knife away and hand me that carving. Yer brother has been taken. Ye don't know where he is or who has him. I do. Give me what I want an' the information is yers."

I wished that I had the Templar's sword to cut off his head and still the words. He would never let me live if the carving was his. He was a viper — out for himself and for the goods and land the Bruce would provide, if he were able to overthrow the English. I saw that now.

Drop the blade. Ye are no match for me. He will not save ye this time. The whisper spread over me. He was strong, his command of the power more sure and skillful than mine. I had the overwhelming desire to do what he asked.

Then, in the back of my mind I heard Aine's hum, and with everything in me I latched on to it. The vision crashed over me with a force that nearly took me to the ground as Aine pulled me into her read of the land over which she was traveling.

The familiar shape of man and horse. The sword I would recognize anywhere. The Templar. In Scotland. Alive. Following a group on horseback.

Torquil.

Gaylen took the opening he had been waiting for and focused the power on me.

ENCROACHING DARKNESS

Wave after wave of power blasted through my shielding as if it were naught. The ground rose up to meet me and the carving tumbled from my grasp as I landed.

The carving! Gaylen! I shouted in my mind.

Forget him. Ye must take our strength, Tormod. The Templar's voice was close, but nothing I could do would break the flow of the power searing my mind and body. Aine's hum played at the edge of my senses. Words accompanied the music and I clearly heard her prayer, *Hail Mary, full o' grace . . . Please, Lady, spare him. I beg o' ye.*

We are nearly there, Tormod, said Bertrand as my mind spun in endless circles of pain. *Hold on. Just a bit longer.* I felt Aine whisper the power, but my mind would not settle. It battered against my skull like a trapped bird seeking freedom. It continued to grow, and I felt my grasp of the here and now fade. The pain was too intense. I could stand it no longer. It had to end, the faster the better. And with a final apology to the Lord, Aine, and the Templar, I gave myself over to the torment, pulling the power to me, willing it to build and grow. *Let it come,* I thought. End my torment.

No, Tormod. Ye're calling it to ye. Press it away! Aine's voice was hardly a flicker of sound in my ears. There was peace offered in the flow of the power that washed through me. I could lose myself. I could let it all go.

The door burst wide and cold air I could hardly feel rushed into the room. Darkness was fast approaching. I willed it to come.

But then, I felt Aine's hands on me and the smallest bit of chaos and insanity dropped away. "Tormod! Don't ye do it. Don't ye dare leave me," Aine sobbed.

I could not see her. I could barely feel her. Then another set of hands pressed to the sides of my head. "Use the power, Tormod." I could hear Bertrand's voice both in my head and in the hut. "Let it go, Tormod. Let the power flow through yer connection to the carving." Bertrand was strong, his healing gift directing me in a way that I could understand. Like a never-ending wave, I felt the surge of power move through me and into the carving, and when it flowed back to me along our bond, it was not the raw danger that it had been. Now it was a healing river of light.

THE CHOICE TO LIVE

As my burned, damaged insides began to repair themselves, visions chased my dreams.

The Templar carried from the cave by Ahram. A land of sand and strange dwellings where he recovered. A ship at sea. Alexander at the helm, his broadsword gleaming.

I resurfaced as if I were struggling from the depths of the ocean. "He's alive, Aine." My voice was raw and I fought to be heard. "Alexander lives."

"Right now, I have to say I am more pleased that ye are alive." Her face was smudged with tears and a feeling that I could not put words to pulsed between us.

"Gaylen?" I whispered, knowing the answer even before I asked.

"He was gone before we arrived," said Aine.

I buried my head in my arms. "He's taken the carving. I've failed in my duties."

I felt her empathy. "But ye kept him from taking the bowl. I could see ye in the tunnels, but to contact ye was not easy."

I nodded. "I thought it would be safer. I'd like to think that the King will never have the whole, but already I've placed one piece into his hands."

"Ye did all ye could. Ye nearly died." She shivered.

"I'm glad ye're all right." I slid my hand up and cupped her head, probing the site of the injury. Her ringlets of short red curls filled my fingers. "I'm so sorry."

She leaned into my hand, rubbing her head against it as if she were a cat. "Bertrand healed me. There's no trace o' injury to be found," she said in wonder.

I smiled.

"An' ye? Are ye well?" she asked.

I didn't answer, just drew her head down until our lips met gently. I kissed her then, and it was even better than before.

EPILOGUE

Bertrand and I returned to the preceptory early the next day, while Aine and my mam got acquainted. It was strange to suddenly reappear at the gates, especially knowing that the Templars had more than likely been searching for me all of the eve, but Bertrand was a strong ally.

Within a candle mark, I was in the infirmary surrounded by a team of high healers who were most intrigued to investigate the solid link that now pulsed healthily inside me. I was poked and prodded and my inners probed until I was ready to scream with frustration.

Gaylen was getting away and I was trapped on a pallet and treated like a bairn, but Bertrand had insisted. Light was waning now in the empty infirmary, and I tossed and turned, trying to find a spot that was less uncomfortable than any other and not succeeding very well. I closed my eyes and reached for the one person who would understand, perhaps the only one feeling more confined than me.

Aine?

It took no more than a moment for her to respond. *I'm outside the gate with a spare set of clothes. Hie yer tail out o' there. We need to leave afore yer mam knows I've gone.*

My laugh was loud in the quiet of the room and I quickly stuffed it back from where it had come. Quietly, I slid from the pallet and began gathering power to whisper the guards. As I stepped from the room, I nearly bumped into the dark silhouette standing against the wall outside the room. Though I hadn't expected him, I was not surprised to see him there. I felt his whisper join my own, and silently Bertrand and I quit the preceptory.

Aine's eyes grew wide when she realized that I was not alone. "Well, what are we going to do?" she asked.

"Hunt down Gaylen, steal back the carving, find the Templar, an' rescue my brother," I said.

She snorted. "Oh, if that's all, then I guess we'd best be off to it then."

Bertrand and I laughed and it felt good. There was much to do, and I still knew I had botched a good deal badly already, but with God's blessing I had faith that once again, perhaps very soon, I would be a Templar's apprentice.

THE END

AUTHOR'S NOTE

Everyone should have a guardian angel. I have many. Thank you, one and all. Beth, Gil, Dan, Grace, the men of Station I, especially Lieutenant Austin and Firefighter Jellison, and all the cardiac and intensive care doctors and nurses at Salem Hospital and Mass General. And I cannot discount my dad and brother.

I hope you enjoyed the second tale in this series. I am having an amazing time combining fiction and history and working the threads of the many underlying strands together. Please excuse any liberties I have taken, particularly the parts with Robert the Bruce. I do not, and never would impugn his honor, I promise.

Thanks of course go out to my editors, Andrea Davis Pinkney and Cassandra Pelham, without whom I would not have come to this fabulous place of plot and intrigue, and to Kim Biggs, who is always there to point me in the right direction. To Amanda, who got shorted in the promise of a dedication by my cardiac arrest, I must once again promise, your day is coming. Aine is you, babe, strong and stubborn. To my men, as always, I love you with all of my heart.